A HERBIE FISHER NOVEL

Barely Legal

Stuart Woods
and Parnell Hall

THORNDIKE PRESS
A part of Gale, a Cengage Company

Farmington Hills, Mich • San Francisco • New York • Waterville, Maine
Meriden, Conn • Mason, Ohio • Chicago

GALE
A Cengage Company

LIBRARY OF CONGRESS CATALOGING-IN-PUBLICATION DATA

Names: Woods, Stuart, author. | Hall, Parnell, author.
Title: Barely legal / by Stuart Woods and Parnell Hall
Description: Large print edition. | Waterville, Maine : Thorndike Press, a part of Gale, a Cengage Company, 2017. | Series: a Herbie Fisher novel | Series: Thorndike Press large print basic
Identifiers: LCCN 2017028664 | ISBN 9781432839246 (hardcover) | ISBN 1432839241 (hardcover)
Subjects: LCSH: Large type books. | BISAC: FICTION / Action & Adventure. | FICTION / Suspense. | FICTION / Thrillers. | GSAFD: Suspense fiction. | Adventure fiction.
Classification: LCC PS3573.O642 B37 2017b | DDC 813/.54—dc23
LC record available at https://lccn.loc.gov/2017028664

Published in 2017 by arrangement with G. P. Putnam's Sons, an imprint of Penguin Publishing Group, a division of Penguin Random House LLC

Printed in the United States of America
1 2 3 4 5 6 7 21 20 19 18 17

BARELY LEGAL

1

Benny Slick's life was flashing before his eyes. It was flashing upside down because two goons were hanging him by his heels from the window of his fourteenth-floor office. The elderly bookmaker had been hit with financial reversals. A horse running at two hundred to one had finished first; a surprising number of people had bet on the nag to win, and in order to pay them off, Benny had been forced to borrow more money than he had any realistic hope of repaying.

The result was a visit from the one man in the world you didn't want to see. Mario "Payday" Capelleti, so named for his habit of walking into the shops of those who owed him money with two thugs and proclaiming "It's Payday!," had quite a reputation, and it wasn't good. Those who didn't pay were left with a reminder of why this behavior might not be the wisest course of action.

Benny Slick was receiving such a reminder.

Mario Payday was puffing on a big cigar. He walked over to the window and blew smoke in Benny's direction. It barely reached him, but the effect was chilling.

"Hi, Benny. Remember me? You should. You took my money. And you failed to pay me back. Not only did you fail to pay me the principal, you failed to pay me the vig. No one fails to pay Mario Payday the interest on a loan. How could you forget that?"

"I didn't forget!" Benny cried desperately.

Mario's eyes narrowed. "You mean you did it deliberately? Benny, you know such disrespect cannot be tolerated."

"I didn't do it deliberately!"

"But you do remember that you owe me money?"

"Yes, yes, I remember."

Mario smiled and spread his arms. "He remembers. It's amazing how quickly people remember when they're upside down. So where is my money?"

Benny's life was still flashing before his eyes, but then he was ninety-two years old and there was a lot to flash. From somewhere in the deep recesses of his mind the right image emerged. "I got it!"

"What have you got, Benny?"

"I got your money!"

"How much money have you got, Benny?"

"I got ninety grand!"

Mario nodded approvingly. "Pull him up."

Mario's goons pulled Benny back into the office. His legs were weak and he could barely stand.

Mario's glare was not helping. "Ninety grand, Benny? You have ninety grand and you couldn't pay me?"

"It's not in cash."

Mario snapped his fingers, pointed to the window. "Put him back."

Benny put up his hands. "No, no, no. You don't have to do that. I have a marker for ninety grand. It's good as cash. You can have it."

"What marker?"

"Vinnie the Vig owed me money, and he didn't have the cash so he gave me a marker."

"Vinnie the Vig is dead."

"It's not his marker. Vinnie was holding another guy's marker for ninety grand. When he went into my debt, he transferred the marker to me, and I will now pass it on to you."

"You have a marker for ninety grand and you never cashed it?"

"I couldn't. I was in prison."

"Where's this marker now?"

9

"It's in my desk." Benny hurried to his desk and began rifling through the drawers, praying he could find the marker he'd promised was in them. He hadn't cashed it because he'd forgotten it was there. Shortly after he'd received it he was sent off to the state penitentiary for indulging in his chosen profession. By the time he got out he'd forgotten all about the marker, and only recalled it with eternity staring him in the eye.

Benny pulled out his petty cash box, took out the money tray, and searched through the papers in the bottom.

Mario watched him with growing skepticism. "You have a marker for ninety grand and you keep it with the petty cash receipts?"

Benny hoped he did, but it was looking less likely.

And then, suddenly, victory.

Benny clutched the slip of paper and held it up. "Here! Here!"

Mario took the marker. "All right, let's see who owes me ninety thousand dollars."

He held it up, read the name.

"Herbie Fisher."

2

Stone Barrington and Dino Bacchetti were having dinner at Patroon, one of their usual haunts since Elaine's had closed. Their entrées had just arrived when Dino looked over Stone's shoulder and his eyes widened. "Uh-oh."

"What?"

"Look who's here."

Stone was contentedly inspecting his steak. "I'm busy. Who is it?"

"Herbie Fisher."

"Oh, great."

"Not necessarily."

"Oh?"

Stone turned and looked. The young man approaching their table was indeed Herbie Fisher. He was impeccably dressed in a suit and tie. He looked like a corporate lawyer, which indeed he was.

Herbie Fisher, the youngest lawyer ever to make senior partner at Woodman & Weld, was a shining star, as adept at attracting clients as he was at handling their legal problems. It was hard to believe he had once been Stone's client, and not in the most savory of cases. Were it not for Stone's legal gymnastics, Herbie probably would have been in jail.

Stone had taken Herbie under his wing, and the young man had flourished under his mentorship. Not only had he straightened out his life, but Stone had taught him where to buy the right suits, where to get the right haircut — in short, how to be a respectable member of high society.

Since turning his life around, Herbie had never caused Stone a moment's concern. On the contrary, he was the attorney to whom Stone was most likely to refer important clients.

At the moment Herbie was grinning from ear to ear, and the cause was undoubtedly the young woman with him. Her beauty was enough to turn any man's head. Though as conservatively dressed as any third-grade schoolteacher, her radiant smile exuded more than a hint of mischief.

Herbie ushered her up to the table.

"Herbie," Stone said.

Herbie shot him a look. Since joining the law firm of Woodman & Weld he had adopted a less juvenile appellation.

Stone quickly corrected himself. "Herb. And who is this charming young lady?"

Herbie positively beamed. "Yvette, these are the men I've been telling you about. Allow me to introduce Stone Barrington and Dino Bacchetti. Gentlemen, this is Yvette Walker, my fiancée."

The young couple exchanged glances.

So did Stone and Dino. It was momentary, however. Then they were greeting Yvette enthusiastically, congratulating young Herbie, and hoping the two would be happy together.

Dino took the lead. "Yvette, I'm so happy for you. How did you meet? Are you a lawyer, too?"

She smiled. "Heaven forbid. I have nothing against lawyers, I just don't want to be one."

"What do you do?"

"I'm an actress."

"Really? What have I seen you in?"

"You probably haven't. I'm just getting started."

"You acted in college?"

"Yes."

"Where did you go?"

"Yale drama school."

Dino smiled. "Well, that's a coincidence.

13

Our sons went to Yale. Ben Bacchetti and Peter Barrington. Perhaps you knew them."

"It's a big school."

"They were in the theater department. Peter got a play produced while he was still in school."

"I know *of* them. Award-winning Hollywood director and the head of Centurion Studios. They were way before my time."

"Not necessarily. Our kids started young."

Yvette's eyes twinkled. "If you think I'm going to tell you my age in front of my fiancée, you can forget it. I've told him just as much as he needs to know, no more, no less. If you prove I'm older than I said I was and he dumps me, I'll sue you for damages."

"And I'd handle the case," Herbie said with a smile. "But that's not going to happen. We're very happy."

"Would you care to join us?" Stone said.

Yvette and Herbie looked at each other. They clearly wished to be alone.

Yvette politely declined. "Thanks, but we've got a lot to talk about. Come on, Herbie."

The happy couple chose a table for two in the back and out of earshot.

"I notice *she* can call him Herbie," Dino said.

14

"Was that nice?" Stone said.

"Was what nice?"

"You were vetting her."

"Was I?"

"You know you were."

Dino shrugged. "Force of habit."

"No, it wasn't. You're suspicious of her."

"Well, can you blame me?"

"What do you mean?"

"Are you kidding me? Ten years ago Herbie was a total fuckup, couldn't tie his shoe. He'd make the worst choices, often endangering his life."

"So?"

"That was nothing compared to his taste in women. He was always showing up with some hooker or other he was madly in love with, despite the fact that he had just met her."

Stone conceded the point. "He even went so far as to marry one."

Herbie's ex-wife had run off to Aruba with her brother, not to mention a few million dollars of company assets, leaving Herbie holding the bag.

"I remember it well. So, here he is, popping up again with a new fiancée. If that's not déjà vu, I don't know what is."

"At least this one isn't a hooker. She looks like a very nice young girl."

15

"I hope so," Dino said.

"You're really concerned."

"Well, I'd hate to see Herbie get his heart broken. Is that bad?"

"It's kind of sweet," Stone said.

Dino threw a napkin at him.

3

On the sidewalk outside Patroon, Mario Payday's goon Carlo leaned up against the window and pressed his face to the glass. The young man at the table in the back certainly appeared to be Herbie Fisher. Of course, it was hard to tell with the picture he had to work with. As usual, in identifying one of Mario Payday's new clients, Carlo had gone right to the source and checked his arrest record. Herbie had one, but his mug shot wasn't very good. The young man in the restaurant looked a lot better than the one in the photo. Of course, at the time the photo was taken he'd just been picked up on a charge of murder, which couldn't have helped. According to the rap sheet, he'd been charged with killing a mobster named Carmine Dattila, commonly known as Dattila the Hun. Carlo remembered the incident. The guy had marched into Dattila's place of business and shot him twice in the head in front of a dozen witnesses. Carlo couldn't imagine the young man at the table doing that. He couldn't imagine *anyone* doing it and beating the rap. Some things, Carlo told himself, just weren't fair.

Carlo whipped out his cell phone and called Mario.

"I got him."

"Got who?"

"Your ninety-thousand-dollar marker. I found him having dinner."

"Where?"

"Patroon. Guy's cleaned up his act some since his last arrest, but it sure looks like him."

"Does he look like he could pay ninety grand?"

"Sure does, unless it's all for show."

"Okay. Make sure it's him. If it is, loosen him up."

"Okay."

Carlo hung up the phone and went in. A man sitting near the door looked familiar, but Carlo couldn't place him. He walked on by and headed for the table in the back of the restaurant.

The young couple were speaking intimately, their heads tilted toward each other, laughing. Carlo would have to spoil their fun. That didn't bother him. Spoiling people's fun was a fringe benefit of the job.

Carlo walked up to the table and said, "Herbie Fisher?"

They looked up.

The girl frowned.

The guy said, "*Herb* Fisher."

Carlo shrugged. "Whatever. Mr. Fisher, you owe me ninety thousand dollars."

The girl was clearly upset. She looked at the young man and said, "Herbie, what's going on?"

"Mister," Herbie said, "I don't know who you are, but I don't owe you ninety thousand dollars."

"Fair enough. You owe my *boss,* and he intends to collect. He wanted me to give you advance notice because he is a very nice guy and likes to give fair warning."

"I don't know what you're talking about. You must have me confused with someone else."

"Herb Fisher? It is Herb Fisher, isn't it?" Carlo slapped the rap sheet down on the table. "This is you, isn't it?"

Herbie got to his feet. "All right. You get the hell out of here."

"Or what?"

"There's no what. You're going to leave under your own power, or I'll have you thrown out."

"Have me thrown out? Oh, big man. What, you gonna call the chef?"

At the table in front, Stone Barrington looked over Dino's shoulder. "Uh-oh."

"What?"

"Looks like trouble."

Dino turned to look. The two men were facing off. "That doesn't look good. You think Herbie would welcome an intervention? Or you think he wants to show off in front of his girl?"

"I'm sure Patroon would welcome an intervention."

Dino got to his feet and started for the back.

Herbie saw Dino and put up his hand. "It's okay. I got this."

Carlo looked to see who was coming up behind him. It was the man who'd been sitting at the front table, the guy who'd looked familiar.

The penny dropped.

It was the commissioner of police!

Carlo shied away from Dino and crashed into Herbie. Herbie grabbed ahold of him to keep them both from going down. Carlo tried to break free, but Herbie had him by the arm. This was not good. Mario would not be pleased if he let himself get picked

20

up by the commissioner of police.

Carlo reached under his jacket and pulled out a snub-nosed revolver.

"Look out, he's got a gun!" Dino yelled.

Herbie spun Carlo away, taking Yvette out of the line of fire.

Carlo's finger twisted around the trigger.

The gun went off.

The sound was deafening in the crowded restaurant.

The bullet missed everyone and plowed into the wall.

The shock of the gunshot made Herbie lose his grip. Carlo spun away, ducked past Dino Bacchetti, and charged down the aisle.

Stone stuck out his foot.

Carlo went down, rolled once, and came up in full panic mode. He fired another shot over his shoulder, lunged out the door, and pelted down the street as if the devil were at his heels.

4

The cops ruined dinner. Any way you sliced it, a romantic evening was not in the offing with ballistics experts digging bullets out of walls and detectives taking witness statements.

The detective taking Herbie's was rather arrogant. His attitude gave the impression he didn't believe a word Herbie said.

Of course, the fact that they had Herbie's rap sheet didn't help.

"The man said you owed him money?"

"That's what he said."

"But you don't?"

"I don't even know who he is."

"If you don't know who he is, how can you be sure you don't owe him money?"

"I don't owe anyone money."

"That's a rather broad statement. Couldn't you have some debt you forgot about?"

"He said I owed him ninety thousand dollars. I'd be apt to remember that."

"And he slapped your rap sheet on the table?"

"That's right."

The detective held it up. "This is your rap sheet?"

"I told you it was. I pointed it out to you."

"You committed all these crimes?"

"Hardly any of them. You'll notice most of the charges were dismissed."

"This one wasn't. Assaulting a police officer."

Herbie said nothing.

"Do I have reason to be alarmed?"

"Only if you scare easily."

"How did you assault the police officer?"

"I kicked him in the balls."

The detective took a step back.

Herbie glanced over at Yvette. She was remaining calm, but he could tell she was less than happy. All this had happened before they even had appetizers, and Yvette had to be getting hungry, because he was.

"Look, guys," Herbie said, "I understand you have to keep me because I had the misfortune of being assaulted in a public restaurant, but there's no reason to punish the young lady, who had absolutely nothing to do with it. Why don't you take a statement from her and let her go?"

"Oh, I'm sorry," the detective said ironically. "Were we inconveniencing you? We wouldn't want to interfere with the dinner plans of you fine folks just because someone showed up at your table and fired a few shots."

Dino Bacchetti cocked his head in the detective's direction. "Sam?"

The detective saw who it was and snapped to attention. "Sir? Did you need something?"

Dino's smile was frosty. "Come here, will you?"

"I think we're about to get the VIP treatment," Herbie whispered to Yvette.

"Oh?"

"Dino didn't like the tone the detective was taking. I think they're discussing proper etiquette now."

"I see."

"I'm afraid it's not going to get us dinner."

"That's all right."

"No, it's not all right. This was our engagement dinner."

"Don't worry. The wedding's still on."

"I'm glad to hear it. Are there any deal breakers involved here? If they lead me away in handcuffs, for instance?"

Yvette's eyes twinkled. "I suppose I should

24

keep my options open. I didn't know you were such a criminal."

"Oh, dear."

"What?"

"Your eyes are sparkling. It's the Robin Hood effect. Girls can't help falling in love with an outlaw."

"Were you really an outlaw?"

"I was just young. And I had no money."

"You stole things?"

"No."

"What did you do?"

"I took borderline jobs."

"Like what?"

"Like taking pictures of a cheating husband with the other woman."

"In bed?"

"I was supposed to."

"What happened?"

"I got arrested."

"Oh?"

"I never said I was a *good* outlaw."

"Oh, dear. Maybe I should reconsider."

"You can if you like. But I'm giving you an engagement dinner, one way or another."

"Just not tonight. Tonight we're having takeout." She favored him with a coquettish smile. "And I'll show my studly little outlaw how lucky he is to be dining at home."

The detective returned in time to hear that.

Herbie found himself blushing furiously.

5

Herbie's clients at Woodman & Weld fell into two categories: those he could tell he'd been shot at in a restaurant, and those with whom it was better he remain silent on the topic.

Joshua Hook fell into the former category. Josh was one of his first clients, right after he'd been made a senior associate at Woodman & Weld. Mike Freeman, the chairman and CEO of Strategic Services, the prestigious defense organization that provided armed bodyguards, state-of-the-art alarm systems, and confidential investigations including the use of spyware, had hired Herbie to set up the corporate framework for Strategic Defenses, a new division that would be wholly owned by Strategic Services but would function as a separate company. Strategic Defenses would specialize in offering bodyguard training to their clients' employees, including the use of firearms, defensive and offensive driving techniques, and the basics of hand-to-hand combat.

Joshua Hook was the ex–CIA agent Mike had hired to be CEO. Herbie hit it off with Josh. They not only set up the school together, but Herbie had taken one of Josh's earliest classes, so he expected to take some ribbing about the shooting.

Sure enough, Josh found it highly amusing.

"I love it," Josh said. "For a defensive training school it's kind of appropriate having an attorney who's a moving target. I hope you took his gun away from him and pistol-whipped him."

"He fled before I could tie him in knots."

"Too bad. We can always use the publicity."

"From what I understand, you're doing quite well as it is."

That was an understatement. Josh's defensive training school was thriving, and even the sprawling facility in upstate New York, which included a high-speed racetrack, indoor and outdoor shooting ranges, and an airstrip, was growing cramped.

Josh had called to see about restructuring the corporation in order to expand. Simple contract work of this nature was something

Herbie would normally have farmed out to an associate, but Josh was a friend, and Herbie always handled Josh's affairs personally.

Herbie had just finished up with Josh when Dino called.

"Hi, Dino. What's up?"

"You busy?"

"I was just on the phone with Josh Hook at Strategic Defenses."

"Oh? How is he doing?"

"Too well. Business is booming, and he needs to expand. He has more students than he can handle."

"Is he still teaching himself?"

"He has a staff of instructors, but he keeps his hand in. There's a waiting list for his classes. Anyway, he wants to restructure, so I have to review the contracts."

"Is that a problem?"

"No, but I need to get it done before brunch."

"Oh?"

"I'm taking Yvette out to make up for last night."

"She'll go for that?"

"What?"

"Trading a dinner for a brunch?"

"She'll get the dinner, too. I'm just *calling* it an engagement brunch. It's the gesture that's important."

"I was kidding. Anyway, about the shoot-ing."

"Any progress?"

"Not really. The bullets are thirty-eight caliber. They don't match the bullets from any crime scene or autopsy or anything we have on file. It doesn't mean we don't have a record of the gun, it just means we don't have any bullets from it."

"That's clear as mud."

"Yeah, it's another way of saying we got nothing. Anyway, you had a good look at the guy. Do you have time to drop by the precinct and look at mug shots?"

"You got a good look. Why don't *you* look at mug shots?"

"I did. Nothing rings a bell. Now, this guy says you owe his boss ninety thousand dol-lars."

"The guy's wrong."

"Didn't you used to have gambling debts?"

"I paid them off."

"Are you sure?"

"Oh, yeah. When I won the lottery, I paid off everybody. Believe me, everybody heard about it and everybody asked."

"There's a bunch of loan sharks around. I'm wondering if any of them might be familiar."

"They're not. The only one I borrowed from was Vinnie the Vig."

"Vinnie the Vig is dead."

"I know. And before he died I paid him every last cent. I tell you, this guy's got me mixed up with someone else."

"Yeah, well, when you come down you can look at their mug shots, too, see if anyone's familiar. So how about it? Can you come over?"

"After brunch."

"I'm going to call and remind you. You got your cell phone? I tried to catch you before but it went to voice mail."

"That's not good," Herbie said. "It's either on silent or I left it at home. Hang on a second."

Herbie snatched up his iPad and opened an app.

"What are you doing?" Dino said.

"Yvette showed me this app — Find My Phone. I call it up on my iPad and I get a map. And the blinking light says . . . it's in my apartment. Great. I'll have her bring it to brunch."

"There's too much damn technology," Dino said.

"I know," Herbie said. "I feel like a dinosaur."

"Join the club."

6

Yvette sipped her cappuccino and smiled at Herbie across the table at the café he had chosen for their engagement brunch. "You didn't have to do this."

"Yes, I did. It's not every bride-to-be who gets shot at instead of eating dinner."

"That makes me special."

"You are special."

Yvette's French toast arrived. She poured on pure maple syrup and loaded a forkful with berries, nuts, and cream. She took a bite and practically purred.

Herbie sliced into his ricotta pancakes and watched her fondly.

"I hope you're not planning a big wedding," Yvette said between bites.

"Of course not. Just two or three hundred of our closest friends."

"I'm serious, Herbie. My parents are dead and I have no close relations."

"We could run off to Vegas if you want."

"Are you serious?"

"Well, if it's over the weekend. We have this corporate merger."

Yvette laughed and shook her head. "Ah, Herbie, you hopeless romantic. Willing to do anything wild and impulsive as long as it fits into Woodman & Weld's schedule."

"It's not so bad, really."

"I didn't say it was bad. I just find it amusing. Oh, I brought your phone." Yvette took it out of her purse and held it up, teasingly. "I'm not sure I should give it to you. You'll just get a call from work."

Herbie smiled. "I told them to hold my calls."

Yvette passed the phone over.

It rang.

"See?" Yvette said. "There's the office now."

"It won't be work," Herbie said. He clicked on the phone. "Hello?"

"Oh, Herb! Thank God I got you! I'm in a terrible bind. I need your help."

"Who is this?"

"It's James Glick."

Herbie frowned. James Glick was one of Woodman & Weld's upcoming young lawyers, but he was a trial lawyer. It wasn't often that trial lawyers needed a corporate consultation, and never urgently and during lunch.

"Yes, James," Herbie said. He tried to keep the irritation out of his voice, but having just told Yvette it wouldn't be someone from the office, he was not in a forgiving mood.

"Oh, I'm sorry. It's the lunch hour, isn't it? I've lost all track of time."

"So, call me later."

"No, no, you don't understand. I need you now. I'm supposed to be in court, but I had to go to the hospital for an emergency appendectomy."

"So call the court and get a continuance."

"I can't. It's Judge Buckingham. You know what he's like. A real prosecutor's judge."

"Wait a minute. This is a criminal case?"

"That's right."

"Why are you handling a criminal case?"

"It's a major client — Councilman Ross."

"The councilman's facing criminal charges?"

"It's his son. College kid, busted for drugs."

"Drugs?"

"Possession of a controlled substance. Possession with intent to sell. Trafficking."

"Trafficking!"

"Not really. They pile on the charges so

they'll have something to plea-bargain. That's all this is. A plea bargain."

"What's the deal?"

"Suspended sentence, community service, the kid walks."

"That's what you're asking?"

"That's what they're offering. It's all set up."

"Why would they offer that?"

"The councilman's a big supporter of the police department. They're happy to cut him a break."

"So all I have to do is appear in court and accept the deal?"

"That's right. Just ask the judge for a recess to talk to the ADA. He'll offer you the deal."

"James, there must be someone you can get better suited than me. I don't work on these kinds of cases at all."

"Not on such short notice. I don't have time to shop around, Herb. I'm calling you from pre-op."

"I was your first choice?"

"No, you were the one who answered the phone. Thanks a million, pal. Just get down to the courthouse. You need to be there by two PM."

Herbie was acutely aware of Yvette's eyes on him. He couldn't bail on her again. Not with her teasing him about being obsessed with his job, and not from their second straight engagement celebration. He was desperately trying to think how to get out of it when James interrupted his train of thought.

"The anesthesiologist just arrived — gotta go! Thanks a million, Herb."

Herbie hung up to find Yvette looking at him with an I-told-you-so smile.

Herbie sighed. "Honey?"

7

James Glick slipped his cell phone back into his pocket. Mr. Glick was on an Amtrak Acela speeding out of New York as fast as the train could carry him. James Glick was not in the hospital, and his appendix was fine. The only part of what he had told Herbie that was true was about being in court at two o'clock. That, and the plea bargain. James Glick had been offered the plea bargain. He just couldn't take it.

Ever since he'd caught the case, James Glick had been pressured by mobsters. The pressure had not been subtle. He'd been muscled into a car and taken to a deserted junkyard on Long Island, where he'd been forced to his knees and a gun had been held to his head. He'd been told to lose the case, and to lose it as quickly as possible, or his next trip to Long Island would be one-way.

As a result he'd waived the probable cause hearing and gone right to trial, assuring his client the prosecution would be eager to do so, too. He hadn't realized how eager until he got into court and was offered such a favorable plea bargain.

The mobsters had stepped in again. This time they hadn't felt the need to drive him to Long Island, they'd simply spelled it out for him. They didn't want him to *settle* the case, they wanted him to *lose* the case, and to lose it badly enough the kid would wind up with a jail sentence. James Glick had no idea why they wanted this, only that they did, and that a dark fate was in store for him if he didn't deliver.

James hated passing the buck to Herb Fisher, but he had no choice. If he took the plea bargain he was dead. Another lawyer might escape such a fate. He wouldn't know what he was up against, and would accept the plea bargain without hesitation. Then there would be no point in killing Herbie, because it would be a fait accompli.

And he would be free of this nagging nightmare. After a while, he might be able to come back. No one knew where he was. They wouldn't be following him.

Or would they? He had a flash of paranoid fear.

He glanced around and saw no one. Of course, he was snug in his seat. He leaned out, peered down the aisle. There was no one in front of him. He glanced behind him. There was no one there.

But that didn't mean they weren't.

Could they have followed him?

They couldn't, could they?

The Acela hurtled down the track.

8

Herbie got to court at 2:05. Ordinarily that wouldn't have been a problem, but apparently in Judge Buckingham's court it was. The judge was already on the bench, and everyone appeared to be waiting for him.

Judge Buckingham had a hawk nose and a perennially stern look. He wasn't drumming his fingers on the desk as Herbie came down the aisle, but he gave that impression.

With a sickening feeling, Herbie realized that he knew him. The judge had presided over one of his many arraignments. Of all the luck.

Charles Grover, a young ADA, was standing next to the prosecution table. Herbie knew Grover, had met him on a case involving the illegal transfer of funds. He and Herbie had managed to work out an equitable solution. At least equitable from Herbie's point of view. Grover had always been of the impression that Herbie had gotten the better of him, which, in fact, he had. Herbie wondered if he still bore a grudge.

Grover caught his eye and smiled. It was, Herbie noted, the smile of a man holding every ace in the deck.

Seated at the defense table was a young man Herbie presumed was his client, a college-age kid, very preppy-looking, with short brown hair and wearing a suit and tie.

Herbie was not one to pigeonhole people, and he had seen criminal lawyers from his firm perform miracles on the scum of the earth with nothing more than a shower, a shave, a haircut, and a clean set of clothes; still, he got the impression his client was the genuine article. Herbie just couldn't imagine this young man dealing drugs. He had an eager, puppy-like quality that couldn't be faked.

"David Ross?"

"Yes?"

"Herb Fisher. Your attorney's in the hospital having emergency surgery. He sent me to fill in."

"Surgery?"

"It's minor. He'll be back." Herbie pointed to his suit jacket. "Did James tell you to wear the suit?"

"No, it's the way I dress."

"Good move. You're a college student?"

41

"That's right."

"What are you studying?"

"Prelaw."

"Well, you're getting an early education."

Judge Buckingham banged the gavel. Herbie looked up to find the judge glowering down at him. "Well, now, nice of you to join us. Where is Mr. Glick?"

"He had an emergency appendectomy, Your Honor," Herbie said.

"Couldn't he have had it after court?"

"No, Your Honor. It was an emergency."

"And who, may I ask, are you?"

That was a relief. The judge didn't remember. "Herb Fisher, Your Honor. Mr. Glick asked me to appear in court and explain his absence."

"You're appearing in his stead?"

"Temporarily. It's minor surgery, and he expects to be back. For that reason, I would ask for an adjournment until tomorrow, at which time Mr. Glick should be able to rejoin us."

"I see no reason for that," Judge Buckingham said, "when he has sent so competent an attorney to function on his behalf. Motion denied."

"Your Honor, I am unfamiliar with the case. Might I have a short recess to confer with my client?"

"I don't see why they couldn't have gotten someone who was familiar with the case."

ADA Grover stood up. "Excuse me, Your Honor, but if you would grant me a brief recess to bring opposing counsel up to speed, perhaps we could expedite this proceeding."

Judge Buckingham nodded. "Excellent idea. Court is in recess for fifteen minutes."

He banged the gavel.

David Ross grabbed Herbie by the arm. "What's going on?"

Herbie put his hand on his client's shoulder. "Don't worry. It's going to be all right. The prosecutor wants to talk to me."

"About what?"

"We'll see. But it must be good."

When they were alone in the conference room, Grover grinned. "How do you like it so far, Herbie?"

"It's Herb these days."

"Whatever," he said dismissively. "I didn't know you were doing criminal law."

"I didn't either. James Glick called me out of the blue. Apparently he couldn't get anyone else."

"Why'd he ask you?"

"I was the first one to answer the phone. I'm still kicking myself."

"Well, don't. It's all worked out. Didn't James tell you?"

"He said to expect a plea bargain. Is that right?"

"Yes, and you couldn't get better terms considering the quantity of drugs involved. Two years' suspended sentence, community service, and the kid walks."

"Why are you offering it?"

"He's the son of a councilman. Councilman Ross is a friend of the police department — no one wants to put his son in jail."

"Just how strong is the prosecution's case?"

"Airtight. The kid was caught with three grams of cocaine in his jacket pocket, individually packaged and ready for sale. Not to mention half a kilo we found stashed in his locker. It's more than enough to convict. It's only natural the kid would cop a plea."

"I suppose."

"Relax. I already worked it out with James Glick. All you have to do is take the deal. So, are we all in agreement? We have a deal?"

"I believe so, but I will have to verify with my client that he wants to accept it."

Grover chuckled. "Are you kidding me?

It's a defendant's dream plea. Of course he's going to take it."

9

"The hell I will!"

"You don't want the deal?"

"Damn right I don't!"

"I was told this was all set up. James Glick, your lawyer, said you had a deal."

"James Glick, my lawyer, never told me anything. This is the first I'm hearing of it."

"You don't want a plea bargain?"

"Who asked for a plea bargain? I don't know where he got that idea." The young man made a face. "I *do* know where he got that idea. It's my father, isn't it?"

"I can't say."

"What do you mean, you can't say? You're my lawyer, aren't you? Are you representing me or not?"

"I'm filling in until your real lawyer returns. I'm attempting to carry out what he started."

"And did he say I asked for a plea bargain?"

"He just told me there was one, and all I had to do was accept it. It's a good deal, David."

"It's a good deal for you. You don't have to do any work. The trial's over, and you can collect a hefty paycheck from my father."

"And you walk, no jail time. You know what the minimums are for drug convictions?"

"Yes, I do, and I'm counting on you to save me from them. Woodman & Weld, big-time lawyers, billing out at I don't even want to know. I was in trouble, and I wanted the best. I didn't expect you to sell me out the moment my dad said boo."

"No one's selling you out."

"You're making a deal behind my back."

"No one's doing anything behind your back. The prosecutor just asked me if we had a deal. Your lawyer told me we did, but I didn't tell the prosecutor that. I said I have to ask my client, he's the only one who can accept a deal. Which is why I'm out here talking to you and taking abuse from the guy I'm trying to help. Do you want to stop impugning my motives so we can both get up to speed?"

Herbie took a breath, blew it out again. "Now, I have not been specifically told, but

I am assuming that your father, horrified that you are on trial and facing jail time, called in a political favor. Which is why you've been offered the best deal a drug defendant ever got since they instituted mandatory minimums. No one's forcing you to take it, but if you're rejecting it just to spite your father, there are a lot easier ways to thumb your nose at your parents than doing five to ten in the state penitentiary."

"I'm not trying to spite my father. I just want to be found not guilty. I'm prelaw. You're a lawyer. You know how tough the competition is for a graduate who just passed the bar. You think I want a drug charge on my record?"

"I'll get the record sealed."

"I don't want the record sealed!"

"You don't want the record sealed?"

"I don't want a record."

"Come on, kid, we live in the real world. Why won't you take a deal?"

David looked him straight in the eye. "Because I didn't do it."

10

Judge Buckingham resumed the bench. "Court is in session. Before the jury is brought back into the room, are there any matters the attorneys wish to bring to my attention?"

ADA Grover was on his feet. "Yes, Your Honor. I believe the defense and the prosecution have agreed on a verdict."

"Is that so, Mr. Fisher?"

Herbie stood up. "I'm afraid not, Your Honor. The defense has no interest in discussing a plea." He added, "We would have no objection to a dismissal or a directed verdict of not guilty, however."

ADA Grover nearly choked. "A dismissal?" he sputtered. "Why in the world would we want to dismiss this case? I —"

Judge Buckingham banged the gavel. "That will do, Mr. Grover. Such outbursts are uncalled for. The court notes your disinclination to dismiss."

"Your Honor," Herbie said, "in light of the fact that this case could not be settled out of court, I would ask for a continuance until such time as Mr. Ross's attorney, James Glick, is able to join us."

"Mr. Glick asked you to act on his behalf?"

"That's right."

"Do it, then. The motion for a continuance is denied. Bring in the jury."

As the court officer went to get the jury, David Ross grabbed Herbie by the sleeve. "What are you going to do?"

"The only thing I can think of."

"What's that?"

"Stall. I'm not going to let the witness get off this stand until court adjourns, and your attorney can take over tomorrow."

"My attorney sold me down the river."

"Your attorney got you a very good deal, but he's not going to force you to take it. And your attorney knows how to cross-examine prosecution witnesses. I've never handled a criminal case before."

"What? Why didn't you say something before?"

"I didn't think I'd find myself in the position that it would matter!"

"Christ."

"Do you want to take the plea bargain?"

50

"No!"

"I've told you my limitations. I've told you what I'm going to do. If you don't like it, fire me, and Judge Buckingham will assign you a public defender."

The jurors filed in and took their places in the jury box. There were fourteen of them, twelve jurors and two alternates.

"Mr. Prosecutor. Call your first witness."

"I call Detective Marvin Kelly."

Detective Kelly was sworn in and took the witness stand.

ADA Grover approached the witness. "Detective Kelly. What is your occupation?"

"I am an undercover agent in the narcotics division of the police department."

"And how long have you been a policeman?"

The detective cleared his throat. "I am a graduate of John Jay College of Criminal Justice. I joined the police force —"

Judge Buckingham interrupted. "This is the point, Mr. Fisher, at which you stipulate Detective Kelly's qualifications subject to the right of cross-examination."

"Yes, Your Honor. So stipulated."

"I'm afraid I can't speak for you, Mr. Fisher. You will have to speak for yourself."

"Yes, Your Honor. The defense stipulates Detective Kelly's qualifications subject to the right of cross-examination."

As ADA Grover nodded thanks to Herbie, his face could not help but betray his amusement.

"Detective Kelly, on the night in question, were you present at a party in a dormitory at Columbia University?"

"I was."

"Were you dressed as a police officer?"

"I was not. I work undercover. I was dressed like someone who might attend such a party."

"As a college student?"

"I'm a little old for that. Perhaps a recent graduate, or a rather hip professor."

"And what did you do at the party?"

"I tried to fit in. I drank and flirted with girls."

"How did that go over?"

"Not bad. Nobody questioned my presence."

"And why were you there?"

"I was acting on information that the defendant was selling drugs at the party."

"So you hung out and mingled?"

"That's right. And conducted a surreptitious surveillance of the subject."

"And what did you observe?"

"The defendant spoke to several students at the party."

"And what did the defendant do on those occasions?"

"He left the room with the person he was talking to and returned minutes later."

"And were you ever close enough to hear what the defendant and the other person were saying?"

"No, I was not."

"Did you personally talk to the defendant?"

"I did."

"What did you say?"

"I asked him where the john was."

The answer drew smiles from the jurors.

"And did he tell you?"

"He was most helpful."

"And did you go?"

"Yes, I didn't want to blow my cover."

"Did you speak to the defendant again?"

"Yes, I did."

"What happened on that occasion?"

"I walked up to him, showed him my identification, and asked him to empty his pockets."

"What did he do?"

"He refused."

Grover raised his eyebrows in feigned incredulousness. "He *refused* to comply with a request from an officer of the law?"

Herbie stirred restlessly. He knew he

couldn't let Grover get away with theatrically underlining the testimony against his client.

"Objection, Your Honor."

"On what grounds?" Judge Buckingham said.

"Already asked and answered."

"Sustained. Mr. Grover, move it along."

"Yes, Your Honor. And when he refused, what did you do?"

"I placed him under arrest and searched him myself."

"What did you find?"

"In his jacket I found an envelope containing three small plastic bags. Each plastic bag contained a gram of a white powdery substance which subsequently proved to be cocaine."

"Did the defendant say anything at the time?"

"Yes. He said, 'That's not mine.' "

" 'That's not mine?' "

"Yes."

"With regard to the envelope you found in his jacket pocket?"

"That's right."

"Was that an outside pocket?"

"No, it was an inside pocket."

"Let me be perfectly clear. The defendant was wearing the jacket at the time?"

"That's right."

"What kind of jacket was it?"

"A sports jacket."

"Like he's wearing now?"

"Yes, only more casual. The one he's wearing now appears to be part of a suit. This was merely a sports jacket."

"But essentially the same type of jacket, with inside breast pockets?"

"That's right."

"And it was in the inside breast pocket that you found the envelope containing the packets of powder?"

"That's right."

"The defendant had the envelope in the front interior pocket of his sports jacket?" Grover shook his head, let the jury share his incredulity. "The envelope of which he said, 'That's not mine'?"

"That's right."

"After the envelope had been removed from his pocket, what did you do with it?"

"I placed it in a plastic evidence bag and wrote my name on it."

"And was that evidence bag sealed?"

"It was."

"What did you do then?"

"I handcuffed him and took him in."

"And did you make any subsequent inspection of the defendant's possessions?"

"I searched his dorm room and his locker."

"What did you find?"

"I found nothing of significance in his dorm room. In his locker, however, I found approximately half a kilo of a substance which later proved to be cocaine."

ADA Grover nodded his approval. "And, going back to the envelope you found in the defendant's jacket pocket, the one containing the three small packets of a white powdery substance. When the defendant said the envelope wasn't his, what did you say?"

"I asked him whose it was."

"And what did he say?"

"He said he didn't know."

Again, ADA Grover let the jury see his skepticism. "He claimed he didn't know whose envelope it was he was carrying around in his pocket?"

"That's right."

"Did you ask him anything else about the envelope?"

"Yes. I asked him what the white powder in the packets was."

"What did he say?"

"He said he had no idea."

"Let me be sure I have this perfectly clear. There was white powder in the gram bags in the envelope in the defendant's interior breast pocket of his sports jacket, and the defendant said he didn't know what it was?"

"That's right."

ADA Grover favored the jury with an incredulous shake of the head before turning to the defense table.

"Your witness."

11

Herbie was momentarily taken aback. Cross-examine a key witness in a criminal case? Where one slipup could send his client straight to jail? Herbie had argued cases involving millions of dollars, but this was something else entirely.

Herbie's adrenaline was pumping furiously, but he couldn't let it show. He took a breath to calm himself, and stepped up to the witness stand.

Detective Kelly stared down at him, smug and superior. From what he'd seen of the lawyer so far, he didn't expect much.

"Detective Kelly, how long have you been a police officer?"

"Eighteen years."

"You studied at John Jay College of Criminal Justice?"

"That's right."

"What did you study?"

"Objection," the prosecutor interjected.

"Relevance?"

"I stipulated Detective Kelly's qualifications subject to the right of cross-examination. I'm cross-examining him on them now."

"Counsel is within his rights. Proceed, Mr. Fisher."

"What did you study at the John Jay College of Criminal Justice, Detective?"

Detective Kelly had his answer ready. "Criminal justice."

His sally drew a laugh from the jurors.

Herbie didn't crack a smile. "And what courses in criminal justice did you take?"

"All of the requirements."

"And what grades did you get in those required courses?"

"Objection."

"Sustained."

"It goes to his qualifications, Your Honor."

"Whether he passed those courses does. The grades he got in them do not."

"And did you graduate, Lieutenant?"

"Yes, of course."

"Were you in the top of your class?"

"Objection."

Judge Buckingham glared down from the bench. Herbie had virtually asked the same question he had just ruled inadmissible. "Attorneys!" he snapped. "Sidebar!"

The two attorneys joined the judge at the side of his bench, where they could speak in low tones out of earshot of the jury. The court reporter carried her typing machine over to take notes on the conversation.

When they had all assembled Judge Buckingham said, "Mr. Fisher, are you trying to annoy me?"

"No, sir."

"You just asked the same question I ruled inadmissible."

"I thought there was a nuance, Your Honor."

"A nuance?" Judge Buckingham said. "It is not your place to find nuances in my rulings."

"I meant in the question, Your Honor."

"I know what you meant, and you know what I meant. It is not your place to get around my rulings by looking for subtle nuances in your questions. If you asked if someone fired a gun, for instance, and I ruled that inadmissible, it would not be admissible for you to ask if that person was holding a gun when it discharged."

"As far as I know, no one has fired a gun in this case."

Judge Buckingham's face purpled. "Your conduct borders on contempt of court, Mr. Fisher. I was giving you a hypothetical

60

example, as you well know. Your remark is improper, as was the asking of your question. You are hereby warned. Should it happen again, you would be in contempt of court."

As he returned to his position at the defense table, Herbie had a smile on his lips. Judge Buckingham had given him a wonderful idea. A sidebar was the perfect way to waste time, and he didn't have to risk contempt of court to get one. Attorneys argued their objections at the sidebar. All he had to do was provoke ADA Grover into objecting to his questions, and he could ask for a sidebar to present his argument of the objection.

Herbie was determined to have as many sidebars as possible.

The fifth time that afternoon the attorneys gathered at the side of the judge's bench to argue an objection, a large, ham-fisted man in the back of the court got up and pushed his way out the doors. He took out his cell phone and called Tommy Taperelli.

"Hey, boss. It's Mookie down at the courthouse."

"Tell me you got good news," Taperelli said.

"Yes and no."

"Don't piss me off. What happened? Did he take the plea?"

"He's not here."

"What!"

"The lawyer didn't show up. He sent another guy in his place."

"Who?"

"Some guy named Fisher."

"All right, did *he* take the plea?"

"No. He left the room to talk to the prosecutor, but they didn't make a deal."

"That's good."

"Yeah. Except the lawyer's not very sharp. Keeps asking a bunch of dumb questions."

"So, he's losing."

"Well, maybe, but he's slow as molasses. The guy's a fucking rain delay. He's still on the first witness, for Christ's sake."

"They're still at it?"

"They're having a sidebar. Which isn't as much fun as it sounds. It's a bar with no booze. A bunch of lawyers talk in low voices so no one can hear, and the jury and the witness just sit there and nothing happens. I thought my head was going to come off. I want to go up there, grab 'em by the collar, say get your ass in gear and do your jobs, for Christ's sake."

"Don't do that, Mookie."

"Never fear. I'm just telling you we don't

have a verdict."

"Well, get back in there and see what we do get."

Taperelli hung up the phone. This was not good. Taperelli was the go-to guy, the guy who delivered. When Taperelli wanted something done, it happened. Most mob bosses were fuckups, as far as he was concerned. Most bosses dressed flashy and cheap. He dressed well. He was elite.

Taperelli had a reputation to maintain. If things went wrong, he'd lose his leverage and the others would move in, and he couldn't afford that. Not if he wanted to keep his political connections and his ties to legitimate business.

From what Mookie had said, things were going very wrong. And worst of all, it had to be on a job for Jules Kenworth.

Taperelli took a deep breath, blew it out angrily, and reached for the phone.

12

Jules Kenworth stood alone in his conference room, gazing down at the huge mahogany table at which he held sway over not just board members but executives, investors, politicians, and would-be bigwigs of all stripes. Kenworth was a mogul's mogul, often imitated, never equaled. He ruled his empire with an iron hand, and had no patience for anyone not on board with his latest venture. His business was real estate. His default mode was acquisition and construction.

The centerpiece of the table was, as always, his current project, in this case the forty-six-story luxury office building he planned for Lower Manhattan. The meticulous scale model, an engineering marvel in its own right, was a beauteous thing to behold.

The phone on the conference table rang. The call must be important or his secretary would not have put it through.

Kenworth picked up the phone. "Yes?" he snapped.

"Tommy Taperelli," his secretary replied.

Kenworth didn't bother to acknowledge her, just clicked the line over. "What?"

Taperelli was used to such briskness from the billionaire developer, and put up with it gladly. Just to be associated with Kenworth upped his stock a hundredfold. Kenworth, on the other hand, was proud of his mob connections. While he would not be caught dead with the likes of Mario Payday, Kenworth was happy to be seen associating with a sophisticated wise guy like Tommy Taperelli.

"I just got a call from court," Taperelli said.

"Don't tell me they took the plea bargain."

"No, but the lawyer didn't show. Sent another guy in his place."

"Any good?"

"No, but he's slow. The case could drag on."

"No good. I want the kid in jail where you can lean on him."

"I know."

"I don't think you do, or I wouldn't be getting this phone call. Let me spell it out for you. Councilman Ross fucked me on

65

this deal and now his kid is going to pay. Because no one fucks me on a deal. No one. I want him in jail, where you can arrange for his 'health benefits' and his 'social calendar,' until his father realizes what a horrible mistake he made. I want him there now. Not next week. Now."

"I know. I know."

"This new lawyer is a problem. I don't want to hear about problems. I just want them to go away."

"I understand."

"I'm glad to hear it. Make the problem go away so I don't get any more of these phone calls."

Kenworth slammed down the phone.

He was righteously pissed. This had to happen, and not just for revenge. Kenworth had practical reasons for needing the kid in jail.

The bone of contention was a zoning ordinance. The councilman had refused to grant an easement on the height restriction on his building, which would have allowed him to add thirty floors. Kenworth stood to lose an astronomical amount if he couldn't change Ross's mind before the council voted next week.

Kenworth shook his head deploringly. Things were getting really bad when you couldn't even trust a mobster to get the job done.

13

Stone Barrington was at the desk in his home office tidying up legal matters when his secretary, Joan Robertson, poked her head in the door. "Dino on three."

Stone picked up the phone. "Hi, Dino, what's up?"

Dino wasn't happy. "I have an ethical problem."

"Wait until she's eighteen."

"Not *that* problem. The detectives investigating the shooting took Yvette's information. I ran it, which I shouldn't have done, I know. But I have, and now the question is — do I tell Herbie what I found?"

"Don't tell me she's a call girl."

"Actually, yes."

Stone laughed.

"What's so funny?"

"Well, it means Herbie is running true to form."

"Yeah, but in this case he doesn't know it

and he's very happy. So what do I do?"

"What do you mean?"

"The question is, should we tell him?"

"Why spoil his fun?"

"You call that fun?"

"Well, it's better than not having a date for the prom."

"You don't think he can interest another woman?"

"That's not the point. He's in love."

"With a hooker."

"Well, nobody's perfect."

"Stone."

"I'm disappointed. Herbie was so happy at dinner. Then he's shot at, shanghaied into court, and his girlfriend's a hooker."

"I could have a talk with her. Maybe she's changed her ways."

"Or you scare her off and break Herbie's heart," Stone said.

"It's going to happen sooner or later." Dino exhaled into the phone. "There's something else."

"What's that?"

"She gave him an app for his iPad — Find My Phone."

"What's that?"

"If you misplace your iPhone, it tells you where it is."

"With a beeping noise?"

"Yeah."

"Can't you just call it?"

"Not if the ringer's off. This thing tells you even if the ringer's off. And if your phone happens to be in the next county, it shows you on a map."

"That's great."

"Yeah, but —"

"But what?"

"Kind of funny thing to give a guy."

"It actually sounds practical."

"Yeah, for her. If she has his iPad, she can open the app and tell exactly where he is at any given time."

"Wouldn't *he* have his iPad?"

"Do you take yours to dinner? So she can check on him. Even if she doesn't have his iPad, if she just has his account and password, she can call it up on hers."

"Why would she need that?"

"I don't know. Maybe so he won't come home while she's boffing the cable guy."

"Oh, gee," Stone said. "Why do you always think the worst of people?"

Dino shrugged. "I'm a cop."

Yvette came out of La Perla with a smile on her lips and a credit card in her purse. Being engaged to Herbie Fisher was a very nice gig. She'd taken the job on, researched

70

it well, knew everything there was to know about the man. Even the fact that he was Herbie Fisher when he won the lottery, and was Herb Fisher now. She called him Herbie, which was a pet name for her, and at the same time a subconscious reminder of the old days before the lottery when he used to be wild. He'd won thirty million. He'd run through half of it, but half remained, plus the generous salary he pulled in from his partnership at Woodman & Weld. If she could just keep him on the string until they were married, she'd be on easy street.

Hell, she was on easy street now. Being engaged to Herbie was a particularly nice job.

Yvette had just stepped off the sidewalk when she felt a hand on her shoulder.

She spun around and gasped. "You!"

The young man grinned. "Hi, sweetie."

"Donnie! What are you doing here?"

"I got lonely."

Whereas Yvette had cleaned up her act for the Herbie sting, her boyfriend, Donnie, hadn't cleaned up his at all. He looked like exactly what he was, a low-life creep.

"Donnie, we talked about this. You have to stay away."

"Why?"

"Because you want money, Donnie. Lots

and lots of money."

"I want some now."

"Soon, sweetie. We're so close."

Donnie grinned, the shit-eating grin she somehow found adorable. "I've had some minor setbacks. You know how it is."

Yvette took a wallet out of her purse. She pulled open the billfold part. She had a hundred and thirty-six dollars. "Here you go, sweetie. Take the hundred, leave me the rest."

Donnie folded the hundred and stuck it in his pocket. He put his arm around her waist. "I'm still lonely."

She twisted out of his grasp. "I know, honey. It won't be long."

"You put that app on his phone, like I told you?"

"Yes, I did, just like you said."

"So where is he?"

Yvette took out her iPhone and turned on the app. "He's in court."

"Excellent," Donnie said. He grabbed her again. "So you have some free time."

"And nowhere to go," Yvette said.

"Don't some of these stores have changing rooms?"

She batted his hand away. "Stop it, Donnie."

"Oh, little Miss Goody Two-shoes." His

face got crafty hard. "Anything you want to tell me?"

"What do you mean?"

"Anything you haven't told me yet? You're so worried I'm going to get careless and blow the gig, I wondered if you had any of the same doubts about yourself."

Yvette practically cooed. "I am playing this so well, honey. He's wrapped around my finger. You wouldn't believe it."

"Anything you're leaving out?"

"No."

"How about getting picked up by the police last night?"

Yvette's mouth fell open. "How do you know that?"

"I know everything. How'd you manage to let that happen?"

"I didn't let that happen. Someone took a shot at me."

"And you couldn't get the hell out of there? You sat and waited for the cops to come?"

"I had to. The commissioner of police was sitting there when the shooting started. Who I'd just been introduced to. I should slip out on him?"

"It doesn't matter what the situation. You never give your name to the police."

"It's all right."

"Oh, yeah? Suppose they pull your record?"

"They won't."

"Why not? They're cops."

"I'm Herbie's fiancée. I'm not a suspect. I was sitting next to him when someone fired a shot."

"Who was it, by the way?"

"I have no idea."

"Who hates the guy?"

"Beats me. Perfectly nice guy." She shrugged. "Of course, he's a lawyer. Lawyers make enemies."

14

Herbie came out of court feeling relieved. He hadn't done any good, but he hadn't done any harm, either. James Glick could take over the cross-examination and it would be as if he'd never appeared. That was okay with him. Herbie was out of ideas, and this was not a case he wished to be associated with. He would be very happy just to be a footnote.

Herbie looked for a cab, though he did not expect to get one. He headed down Centre Street toward the subway at City Hall.

"Herbie Fisher."

Herbie stopped, found himself looking into the face of a muscle-bound goon. Another steroidal specimen stood next to him.

"Yeah?" Herbie said.

"A friend of ours would like to have a little talk."

Herbie exhaled sharply. "Look. It's late, I'm tired, I've had a long day. If you don't mind, I'd just like to get home."

"Ah, but we do mind, Mr. Fisher."

Herbie looked from one to the other. "Gentlemen, it is broad daylight."

The goon shrugged. "So what?" He gestured to a car that had just pulled up to the curb.

"I'm not getting in that car."

The goon shoved a gun in his ribs. "Oh, I think you are, Mr. Fisher. Please don't make me hurt you. The boss won't like it if I hurt you."

Herbie found himself prodded toward the car. Before he knew it, he found himself in the backseat, seated between two thugs. As the car took off, the driver half turned in his seat.

The driver was Carlo, the hood who had accosted him in the restaurant. Herbie recognized him and his mouth fell open.

Carlo grinned. "Don't worry, Mr. Fisher, you're not going to be whacked." After a moment he added, "Yet."

The car pulled up in front of a dilapidated office building on Ninth Avenue in the Thirties. Carlo and another thug marched Herbie through the front door, which was open, and into an elevator in the back. The buttons in it were the type that went out of fashion in the fifties. They were metal, and thick, and stuck out a good inch.

Carlo pushed the button marked 8. It stuck going in. Then the door closed and the elevator lurched upward with an unsettling clanking noise. Herbie had visions of being trapped in the damn thing all night.

The door opened on the eighth floor. They marched him down the hall to a frosted-glass door with the hand-lettered sign FINANCIAL PLANNER. They opened the door and guided him inside.

Seated at the desk was a large man with a round face and a big mustache. He looked vaguely familiar. The man got up and came around the desk. "Herbie Fisher. How nice of you to drop in."

"Who are you?"

"You don't know me? I am hurt, I am wounded, I am cut to the quick."

"You'll get over it."

Carlo punched him in the stomach. Herbie doubled up, gasping for air.

"Carlo, are such theatrics necessary?"

Carlo shrugged. "Seemed like it."

"You were rude to my boy Carlo, Mr. Fisher. Last night, in the restaurant, if you'll recall. Carlo does not take well to rudeness. He has a sensitive nature."

Carlo looked like he bit the wings off flies. Herbie said nothing.

"You may not know me, Mr. Fisher, but I am Mario Payday, so called because every day is payday, and I am the one who gets paid. And you, Mr. Fisher, owe me ninety thousand dollars."

"I don't owe you anything."

Mario sighed. "I must say, you are not the first person ever to feel that way. Others have been of the same opinion until they saw the error of their ways."

"If you will forgive me, Mr. Payday, I have heard of you, of course, but I don't owe anybody ninety thousand dollars."

"You are wrong, Mr. Fisher. You owe it to me."

"No, I don't."

It happened fast. One moment Herbie was standing in front of Mario Payday. The next he was off the ground, flailing in a bear hug. He felt hands on his legs, heard a window open, and suddenly he was a short-range missile, hurtling out into the open air. At the last moment hands closed around his ankles and jerked him upside down, and the next thing he saw was the Ninth Avenue traffic in the street far below. Coins fell from his pockets, any one of which might have killed a passing pedestrian. It occurred to

78

him that he was being shaken. The two men holding him appeared to be playing a game to see which one of them could come the closest to letting go entirely without actually letting him fall.

Mario Payday must have felt that way, too, because the words "Don't drop him" filtered down.

Herbie's original thought, that this couldn't be happening, had been replaced by abject fear, so he found the words reassuring. The big boss didn't want them to drop him, therefore he wouldn't be dropped. He was as safe as any man hanging upside down out an eighth-story window could be.

Then suddenly they were pulling him up, and he was inside the office and back on his feet, and Mario Payday was in front of him, his expression benign and friendly and comforting. It was the most chilling thing he had ever seen.

"Are you all right, Mr. Fisher? You look a bit pale. Do you feel faint? Would you like a drink? Carlo, pour him a drink."

"I don't want a drink."

"Yes, you do. You're coming to your senses. It's always a shock when one comes to one's senses."

"I don't need a drink."

"Sure you do. Give you a moment to recollect."

Carlo shoved a glass of whiskey into Herbie's hand.

"Now, Mr. Fisher, do you recall the ninety thousand dollars you owe me?"

Herbie set the glass on the desk. "The ninety thousand I paid back to Vinnie the Vig?"

Carlo took a step toward Herbie, but Mario put up his hand. "Yes, that ninety thousand, Mr. Fisher. I'm glad you remembered."

"You'll pardon me for asking, but why would an ancient debt to Vinnie the Vig, which I actually paid off, have anything to do with you?"

Mario nodded. "That is a fair question. Do you know how you know it is a fair question? Because you are not hanging out the window for asking it. It appears your marker became collateral in a transaction between Vinnie the Vig and Benny Slick."

"I don't know Benny Slick."

"Maybe not, but he received this marker from Vinnie the Vig shortly before the gentleman's untimely demise." Mario unfolded the marker and held it in front of Herbie's face. "Here's the original marker. Pay to the order of Vinnie the Vig, ninety

80

thousand dollars, signed Herbie Fisher. You can see where Vinnie the Vig crossed out his name, wrote in the name of Benny Slick, and signed it, transferring the debt to him. And here, where Benny Slick crossed out his name, wrote in mine, and signed it, transferring the debt to me."

"It's a worthless marker. I already paid it back."

"Does it say *paid* anywhere, Mr. Fisher? When someone pays off a marker they either take it back or scrawl paid across it. I don't see that here, do you?"

Herbie groaned. In the old days he had not been careful at all about his paperwork. Not getting a receipt for a ninety-thousand-dollar payment was par for the course.

"So, Mr. Fisher. What I want you to remember is, no matter who you think you paid back, you owe the money to me. I'm Mario Payday. I have a reputation to uphold. They don't call me Mario Payday because I have a reputation for *not* getting paid. They call me Mario Payday because I have a reputation for getting paid all the time. You, Mr. Fisher, have the opportunity of helping me to build that reputation. Since you claim you were not aware of this obligation, I am going to be lenient. From the way that you're dressed, it is perfectly clear that you

81

should have no trouble discharging your debt. But just to show you what a nice guy I am, I will forgo the vig. But I want the rest of the debt paid in full by this time tomorrow.

"You have twenty-four hours, Mr. Fisher."

15

Tommy Taperelli was in a very bad mood. He'd been on the phone with his mistress when his wife called him at work, resulting in the nightmare scenario he'd always envisioned of having two women on hold and being in danger of pushing the wrong flashing button and saying the wrong name, resulting in a messy and financially disastrous divorce. He couldn't deal with it, not with the verdict hanging fire and the whole Kenworth business up in the air. His mistress would just have to get off the line. He pushed the button to tell her that, and realized by doing so he had put himself in the nightmare scenario. He hung up on whichever woman was on the line and disconnected the other one. Breathing hard, he leaned back in his desk chair and poured himself a shot of whiskey to settle his nerves.

The phone rang.

Taperelli tossed off the shot and scooped

up the phone.

It was Mookie. "Court's over."

"They got a verdict?"

"No, they quit for the day. I thought it was never going to end."

"Is the trial almost over?"

"Fuck, no. They're still on the same witness. You get the idea the lawyer's just stalling till the other guy gets back."

"When is that?"

"I don't know. He said emergency appendectomy. How long does that take? Kind of a rinky-dink operation, isn't it? I mean, an appendix ain't worth shit."

"This lawyer Fisher. What's his first name?"

"I don't know."

"You know how many Fishers there are in the New York phone book?"

"You want me to count 'em?"

Taperelli slammed down the phone and called James Glick.

The lawyer answered on the second ring. "Hello?"

"Mr. Glick," Taperelli said ominously, "do you know who this is?"

There was a pause, then, "Oh. Hi."

"How come you weren't in court today?"

"My appendix burst. I had to have surgery."

84

"So you'll be back tomorrow."

"Well, that depends on —"

"That wasn't a question, Mr. Glick. You'll be back tomorrow. Right?"

"Right. I'll be back tomorrow."

"You'll be in court, and you'll get a verdict by tomorrow night. Or you know what? You'll wind up right back in the hospital. What hospital you in?"

"Oh, I gotta go, the doctor just walked in," James Glick said, and hung up.

Taperelli stared at the phone. *James Glick* hung up on him? No one hung up on Tommy Taperelli. No one. In the middle of the conversation? Without answering his question? Not only did he not know what hospital James Glick was in, he hadn't had a chance to ask him Fisher's first name.

Taperelli snatched up the phone and called James Glick back.

The call went to voice mail.

Taperelli flung his phone across the room. It clattered against the wall.

James Glick hung up the phone in mortal terror.

Tommy Taperelli knew! Glick was sure of it. He hadn't bought the appendix operation one bit. That's why he'd asked for the name of the hospital. Thank God he'd sent

85

the second call to voice mail. God bless caller ID.

But if Taperelli was on to him, when did he get on to him? And how did he know? Could Herb Fisher have ratted him out? No, not possible. He had been on the Acela when he called Herb Fisher. Even if Herb had tipped him off, Taperelli couldn't get men on the train. And Herb didn't know he was on the train. He was just being paranoid.

James Glick's mind did a backflip. Wait a minute. If Tommy Taperelli wanted him in court tomorrow, Herb Fisher couldn't have taken the plea bargain. If he had, the case would be over and there would be no court to show up in, and Herb Fisher would be hanging by his balls from the nearest construction crane.

James Glick looked up from the sandwich he was trying to choke down in the restaurant in Union Station while he waited for the next train for Miami. Two guys who looked like torpedoes were sitting at a table across the way. They had their chairs angled so they were both facing him.

Glick looked away, willed himself to eat his sandwich and not look back. His resolution lasted a good thirty seconds.

One of the thugs was still looking.

James Glick left his sandwich on the plate and called for the check.

16

Herbie Fisher owned a very nice penthouse on Park Avenue, but the two paintings that adorned the wall of his foyer were probably worth more than the apartment itself. The Picasso and the Braque had been a gift from Eduardo Bianchi, who had left them to Herbie in his will. Eduardo had only known Herbie a short time, but had been fond of the boy, and had placed a great deal of weight in Stone Barrington's approval. Herbie had been shocked and touched by the inheritance, and he displayed the paintings proudly. He fully intended to purchase other art objects, but never seemed to have the time.

As he stepped from the elevator, utterly exhausted from the day in court and his encounter with Mario Payday, he found Yvette standing there clad in nothing but stiletto boots, a sheer negligee, and lingerie that to his experienced eye looked like La Perla.

Yvette thrust a martini into his hand and loosened the ribbon at the neck of the negligee, which fluttered to the floor.

Herbie blinked and gawked. "What the hell."

"Hi, honey," Yvette said. "I was pretending I was the wife in a sitcom welcoming her husband home. Isn't this how they do it?"

Without giving him a chance to answer, she threw her arms around his neck, spilling the martini, and kissed him on the mouth. He scooped her up in his arms and carried her to bed, all thoughts of court and old gambling debts forgotten.

17

David Ross went home to his father's Fifth Avenue apartment. David had a dorm room at Columbia, but his father's apartment was more convenient, being on the East Side like the court. It was also more comfortable. The councilman's floor-through duplex boasted several amenities not available in the dorm room, like food, for instance, and David's own shower and sauna and big-screen TV.

David's father met him in the foyer, which was large enough for the average apartment's living room. It was furnished with a couple of divans and side tables, to handle the slipover from the parties the councilman was sometimes forced to throw.

"What do you mean you didn't take the deal?" Councilman Ross said. "I had it all worked out."

"You didn't tell me."

"I tried to tell you, you didn't listen."

"Because you didn't listen to me. I didn't do it. The drugs weren't mine, and someone set me up."

"This is not the most brilliant defense ever thought of. Any penny ante thief ever busted with the goods says, 'That's not mine.' "

"It's not a story, Dad, it's the truth, and I'll find a way to prove it."

"Didn't your lawyer strongly advise you against doing that?"

"My lawyer wasn't there."

"What?"

"He was in the hospital, so he sent another guy in his place."

"What guy?"

"A lawyer named Herb Fisher."

"How is he?"

"I don't think he's very good, but he isn't forcing me to do anything I don't want to do," David said, and stomped off to his room.

"Oh, for God's sake!"

Councilman Ross prided himself on rarely getting upset. He was a politician's politician, who knew which side of the bread his butter was on. No matter how sticky a situation, he always managed to come out squeaky clean. He'd earned the allegiance of the police department not by any special favors, but by always appearing to be on

91

their side, whether he was or not.

Arranging the plea bargain had not been difficult, just inconvenient. He hated to waste the political favor, but it had been necessary. A misdemeanor settled out of court would scarcely sully his reputation. His son in jail on a drug conviction could have been the nail in his political coffin. Underneath it all the councilman really did love his son and would do anything to save him. He just had trouble letting it show.

The councilman went into his home office and dialed the cell number of Bill Eggers, the CEO of Woodman & Weld.

Eggers was surprised to hear from him. "Councilman. What's wrong?"

"My son's attorney didn't show up for court."

"Impossible. I'd have heard about it."

"He sent a replacement. Can you believe that? A substitute. This is my son, for Christ's sake."

"Who'd he send?"

"Herb Fisher."

"Councilman, this is actually very good news. James Glick is an excellent courtroom lawyer, which is why I assigned him to your son's case, but Herb Fisher is a brilliant attorney and a partner in the firm. Trust me, you could not be in better hands."

"So you say. He rejected the plea."

"He what?"

"He rejected it. Against my express orders."

"That's the first I've heard of it."

"It's the first *I've* heard of it. I'm waiting for my son to come home a free man and he's still on trial."

"Relax. I'll get to the bottom of this." Bill Eggers broke the connection and called James Glick.

18

James Glick's cell phone rang on the platform of the Metro station. He'd been scared out of the restaurant by the two torpedoes and was riding the subway a few stops just to make sure they weren't following him. He jerked the phone out of his pocket and glanced at caller ID.

It was Herb Fisher. That was a surprise. He'd half expected Herb to be at the bottom of the East River.

"James, it's Herb Fisher. How'd the surgery go?"

"Great, great!" James blurted, his mind in chaos.

"So there's no complications. You'll be back in court tomorrow?"

"Oh. Complications. Yes. Well, the surgery went well, but I've developed a post-op infection, they're probably going to keep me."

"You're not going to be in court?"

"Sorry about that, but you know how these doctors are."

"No, I don't know how these doctors are. This is not what I bargained for, James. I can't handle a criminal case. You got me cross-examining the key witness, for Christ's sake."

"I don't understand. Why didn't you take the plea bargain?"

"The client doesn't want it."

"The client's a kid. His father set up the plea bargain. It was all worked out."

"The kid's a legal adult. His father can't plead him out."

"You were supposed to make him want it."

"You neglected to tell me that. Now I'm in court trying the damn case. The prosecution led off with the detective who found the drugs on the kid. If we can't break that down, how do we beat the charge?"

"We cop the damn plea!"

"The kid didn't take the plea. The detective testified. I'm asking him everything but his shoe size until you get back and take over, so you better get back and take over."

"If the doctor says I can't, I can't. They got more rules here than the county pen."

James Glick hung up the phone in mounting confusion. Taperelli wasn't setting him up. Taperelli was telling the truth. The case hadn't been settled. Herbie Fisher hadn't taken the plea. The proof of that was that Herbie Fisher was still alive.

His cell phone rang again. He jerked it out of his pocket, checked caller ID.

Bill Eggers.

If he ever wanted to work again, he'd better take the call.

He clicked the button, adopted a weak, coming-out-of-anesthesia, barely-able-to-speak voice. "Yes."

"Where are you?"

"I had surgery."

"That's what I hear. Not from you, the person I should be hearing it from, but from Councilman Ross. Do you know how stupid it makes me look when someone tells me something about my firm that I don't know?"

"It was an emergency."

"Are you going to be in court tomorrow?"

"If my doctor lets me."

"What's his name?"

"It's a foreign name. And —"

James Glick's heart nearly stopped. The two torpedoes had just come down the escalator and stepped onto the platform.

"Oh shit!" he exclaimed, dropping his phone on the concrete. He scooped it up,

96

clicked it off, and headed down the platform.

There was no exit at the other end.

And the men were coming.

Before they reached him a train pulled into the station. The doors hissed open.

He tried to see if the men got on, but there were too many people in between.

James Glick was stuck. Getting on the train with the two men would be bad.

Being left alone on the platform with them would be worse.

James Glick took a deep breath and stepped inside, just as the doors closed behind him.

19

Bill Eggers called James Glick back, but James sent it to voice mail. He tried three more times before he called Herbie Fisher. By then he was somewhat worked up.

"Herbie?"

"Herb."

"I'll call you any goddamned thing I want. It's my firm and I'm the boss. You may be a good lawyer, but you're making waves."

"The councilman's kid?"

"You got any other case you're fucking up? I thought you weren't doing trial work."

"I'm not. It was an emergency. I had to go to court."

"All you had to do was show up. You shake hands with the ADA and the kid walks."

"The kid didn't see it that way."

"It's important. I need this handled."

"Put someone else on the case."

"I *can't* put another lawyer on the case! I just got through telling the councilman *you* were the best we had. If I pull you off the case, Ross would have my head. We'd lose every client he's ever shaken hands with, and he's a politician. They shake hands a lot."

"What do you want me to do?"

"Get back in court and fix this."

"How?"

"Get the kid to take a deal."

"And if he won't take it?"

"Start printing your résumé."

Dino and Viv were sharing a quiet moment in bed watching TV. It was a rare event that neither of them was busy. They'd spent the evening making love, and were enjoying the afterglow.

The phone rang.

Dino frowned at having his evening interrupted, but seeing Herb's name on caller ID, he decided to pick up.

"Hi, Herb. Still worried about being shot at?"

"Hadn't occurred to me. Do you happen to know a narcotics detective by the name of Marvin Kelly?"

"What about him?"

"Is he dirty?"

Dino blinked. "You call me up in the middle of *The Daily Show* to ask me if one of my detectives is dirty?"

"It's not a casual question, Dino. I got fucked into handling a criminal case, and

I've got a college-age kid facing jail time if I can't save him, which I'm ill equipped to do. Kelly's the key witness, so if he's got a weakness, I need to know."

"Is this a good kid?"

"Yeah."

"Do you want me to make a phone call, see if there's something can be done?"

"The kid's already rejected a plea bargain. I was supposed to walk into court and accept it, but the kid refused to accept the plea, says he's innocent, and now I'm on the hook."

"What was he caught with?"

"Half a kilo of coke."

"What was the deal?"

"Two years' suspended sentence, community service, and the kid walks."

"Are you kidding me? And you kicked that deal in favor of badmouthing one of my cops?"

"I wanted to take the deal. The kid turned it down."

"So beat some sense into him."

"The kid makes a good case, Dino."

"What's that?"

"Why should he take the plea if he's innocent?"

"What makes you think he's innocent?"

"The fact that he won't take the plea."

"Oh, for Christ's sake. What are you, a fucking idealist? We live in the real world, Herbie. Sometimes something is wrong and you can't fix it. Sometimes you have to do something else so it evens out. Kid getting framed isn't fair. Kid walking on a drug charge isn't fair. It's a wash."

"You want to come down to court and tell him to take the plea? Maybe hearing the commissioner of police explain the pragmatism of law enforcement would have more effect."

"Fuck you, too, Herbie."

Dino hung up the phone.

Viv was about to snap the TV back on when she saw the look on his face. "What's the matter?"

Dino sighed. "Ah, hell." He picked up the phone. "Sorry to bother you this time of night. Get me everything there is to know about a Detective Marvin Kelly."

21

Dino met Stone for breakfast. Stone had been surprised to get the call. He and Dino often had lunch or dinner, but not often breakfast. Stone figured Dino had something on his mind.

Stone had just taken his seat when Dino walked in, looking agitated.

"Do you mind if I have Herbie whacked?" Dino inquired.

"What's he done now?"

"He called me last night to ask if one of my cops was dirty."

"Is he?"

"I can have more than one person whacked, you know," Dino said with a meaningful look.

"Who is he?"

"Detective Kelly, Narcotics."

"Do you know about him?"

"I know about all my officers. That's what being commissioner is all about."

"I'll see you get a letter of commendation."

"I'd prefer a cash kickback."

"May I quote you on that?"

"If you want your car ticketed and towed every time you park it."

"Fred stays in the car when it's parked."

"Then you'll also have to bail him out."

"I get the feeling you're bantering to avoid talking about Detective Kelly."

"Good guess. Detective Kelly is the type of cop that gives other cops a bad name. It's not just that he's dirty. He flaunts it. He's connected to Tommy Taperelli, a bigtime mob boss. Does him favors, helps him out of tight spots, looks the other way. He has other unsavory connections, but Taperelli's the biggest."

"And you want to whack Herbie for asking if the guy is dirty?"

"Well, I can't kill Taperelli."

"What's his story."

"High-class mobster, big-time racketeer. He runs a trucking business and handles the import-export of a number of items, many of them legal. The few that aren't fund the rest. He claims he's not into drugs, but any number of the bosses he runs are. Meanwhile, he keeps his hands clean and has ties to several politicians and big businessmen. Prides himself on his connections. Conversely, prominent people pride themselves on being connected to him. Having a Vice cop in his pocket is no surprise. It's his standard MO."

"Did you tell Herbie?"

"Of course I did. He could get killed messing around with goons like Taperelli."

"He's got more sense than that."

"He does now. I seem to recall him walking up to a mobster by the name of Dattila in broad daylight and shooting him twice in the head."

"He was justified."

"Yeah, and he'd be dead if the police hadn't raided the place and disarmed all of Dattila's men an hour before. Herbie didn't know that, and he did it anyway."

"He's a different person now."

"He's engaged to a hooker . . . again."

"Why's he still in court?" Stone said, sidestepping Dino's point. "I thought he was just filling in for one day."

"The lawyer had complications that are keeping him in the hospital. Herbie's on the hook."

"What's Detective Kelly to him anyway?"

"He's the witness Herb's going to cross-examine."

"Herbie's going to walk into court and try

to prove he's a bad cop?"

"I'm afraid so."

"Is that safe?"

Dino shrugged. "I guess we'll find out."

22

Herbie got to court to find that reinforcements had arrived. Unfortunately, they were not in the form of James Glick, but rather his client's father, who seemed more likely to horsewhip the boy than offer any source of comfort. The councilman managed to tear himself away from haranguing his son long enough to demand why Herbie had rejected the plea bargain he had worked so hard to set up, whereupon his son jumped in saying he was the one who had rejected it, and the whole merry-go-round began again.

Having observed Herbie's entrance into the building, Mookie went outside and called Taperelli. "The lawyer's here."
    "Which one?"
    "Fisher."
    "What about Glick?"
    "He's not here."

"Shit."

"His name's Herb."

"What?"

"The lawyer. His name's Herb Fisher."

"Right."

Taperelli already knew that. He'd called the firm first thing in the morning and asked for an attorney named Fisher. The switchboard girl said, "We have a Herb Fisher, but he's not in yet." Taperelli had hung up, hoping that meant the man was coming into the office and not going to court. No such luck.

"You want me to talk to him?"

"Fisher?"

"Yeah."

"Not in court. When they break for lunch."

"Should I lean on him?"

"Depends what he does in court. If he keeps stalling, give him a talking-to. If he takes a dive, let him go. If you're not sure, call me."

"Gotcha."

"Whatever you do, call me."

"What if they decide to take a plea?"

"Shoot him in the fucking head."

23

Herbie waited until his client's father had taken a seat in the gallery before resuming his place at the defense table.

Before he could even sit down, David tugged him by the sleeve. "I thought of something."

"What's that?"

"The detective testified that he searched me and found the cocaine. Like he found the envelope, and took it out of my pocket."

"Yeah. So?"

"That's not what happened. When he put me under arrest he told me to empty my pockets. I did. *I* took the envelope out of my jacket pocket."

"Is that right?"

"Yeah. So if my fingerprints are on it, that's why."

"Interesting."

Judge Buckingham took his place on the bench and regarded the defense table with some displeasure. "Well, Mr. Fisher, it appears you are still with us. I trust you are prepared to soldier on."

"I will do my best, Your Honor."

"God save us."

Judge Buckingham gaveled court into session. The bailiff brought in the jury, and Detective Kelly returned to the stand.

"Detective, I remind you that you are still under oath. Proceed, Mr. Fisher."

Herbie stepped up to the witness stand. He felt rather small. The detective looked arrogant as ever, and the judge was doing little to conceal his bias. And now he had the disapproval of the councilman boring into his back.

"Detective Kelly, do you consider yourself an experienced detective?"

"I do."

"You've busted people for drugs before?"

"Yes, I have."

"And you've testified in court on other occasions?"

"That's right."

"You feel that you would have an opinion in these matters that the jurors could trust?"

"Yes, of course."

"Then let me ask you this — do you think the defendant is innocent?"

Detective Kelly was startled. He could

hardly believe Herbie had asked him that. He paused before answering. "No, I do not."

"You think he's guilty?"

"Yes, I do."

"On what do you base that opinion?"

"On the evidence that I collected as a veteran police detective."

"On the evidence that you collected? Good. Let's look at that evidence. I believe you found an envelope with packets of cocaine in the defendant's jacket."

"That's right."

"Did you find any fingerprints on the envelope?"

"Yes, I did."

"And whose fingerprints were they?"

"They were the fingerprints of the defendant, David Ross."

"Did you find anyone else's fingerprints on the envelope?"

"No, I did not."

"You found only the defendant's fingerprints?"

"That's right."

"Indicating that he was the only one who had touched that envelope?"

"That's right."

"Did you find the defendant's fingerprints anywhere else?"

Detective Kelly frowned. "What do you mean?"

"Pertaining to the case. Did you find his fingerprints on the packets of cocaine inside the envelope?"

"No, I did not."

"You found no fingerprints at all?"

"On the packets, no."

"Getting back to the envelope. As I recall your testimony, you asked him to empty his pockets and he refused, is that right?"

"That's right."

"Then you placed him under arrest and searched him. Did you take the envelope out of his pocket?"

"Yes, I did."

"Then why aren't your fingerprints on it?"

"I'm a veteran detective. I don't contaminate evidence."

"Were you wearing gloves? I wouldn't think so, because you were undercover at the party, and gloves are pretty much a dead giveaway. I would think you were bare-handed when all this was happening, were you not?"

"I was barehanded until I was aware of a crime. When I was, I pulled on a pair of gloves which I had in my pocket, and processed the evidence."

"And you became aware there was a crime

when you found evidence of drugs in the defendant's pocket, did you not?"

Detective Kelly said nothing.

"Well, if you had reached in his pocket with your bare hand, your fingerprints would be on that envelope, would they not? I suggest, Detective Kelly, that when you placed the defendant under arrest, you ordered him to empty his pockets and he did, in fact, comply. He reached in his pocket and took out the envelope, which he was surprised to see there. Is that perhaps how it happened, Detective Kelly?"

"No, it is not."

"The defendant took the envelope out of his pocket, and that is why his fingerprints are on it and yours are not."

"Objection. Argumentative."

"Sustained."

"Detective, you testified that you found half a kilo of cocaine in the defendant's locker, is that right?"

"That's right."

"You seize a lot of cocaine in your drug busts, do you not, Detective?"

"Yes."

"And what happens to the cocaine that is seized?"

"It is logged, sealed, and stored in the evidence room."

"The evidence room?"

"Yes."

"And who has access to the evidence room?"

"There are six policemen in charge of the evidence room. They work in shifts. Someone is at the desk at all times."

"The desk?"

"Yes."

"And what do they do at the desk?"

"They sign evidence in."

"And sign evidence out?"

"There is no need to sign evidence out."

"Really? Aren't you asked to bring evidence into court?"

"Well, that's different."

"How is that different?"

"That's signing evidence out for a reason."

"What about signing evidence out for no reason?"

"I don't understand."

"Well, you said that signing evidence out for court is signing it out for a reason. When, Detective, would you ever sign it out for no reason?"

"I wouldn't."

"And if I were to produce a witness who would testify that you signed out half a kilo of cocaine and never signed it back in, that witness would be mistaken?"

Detective Kelly was unruffled. "Absolutely."

Herbie frowned. He was getting nowhere, and the detective was shrugging off his questions. It was time to go for it.

Herbie took a breath. "Detective, are you familiar with a man named Tommy Taperelli?"

"Objection, Your Honor. Relevance?"

Herbie had been watching Kelly's face. The witness was clearly jolted by the question. "I can connect it up, Your Honor."

Judge Buckingham shook his head. "The connection should come first. Sustained."

"Yes, Your Honor. Detective, has Tommy Taperelli in any way influenced the testimony you are giving here today?"

"Objection!" Grover thundered.

And the court went wild.

24

Mookie didn't care how long it took to straighten this one out, he slipped out and made the call.

"Give me good news," Taperelli said.

"Can't do it. The news is pretty bad. Fuckin' attorney must have had a steroid shot. He came out of the gate like a new man. In fact, he's doing pretty damn good."

"How good?"

"He's got the detective on the run. The prosecutor's running scared and keeps objecting, but he's pissing the judge off, and that's not good. The judge keeps calling sidebars and chambers and sending out the jury. It's still taking forever, only now it looks like they could win."

"Oh, for Christ's sake. Do I have to come down there and handle this myself?"

"No, don't do that. The lawyer asked the witness flat out if Tommy Taperelli was telling him what to do."

"He didn't!"

"He did. And the prosecutor objected and they're arguing about it, but if you show up in court they'll think you *do* have something to do with it."

"Wouldn't I be interested enough that my name came up in cross-examination?"

"Yeah, but if you know it did, you must be keeping tabs on the trial, and that's not good."

"Sometimes you're not so dumb, Mookie."

"So, you want me to lean on him?"

"You might have a little talk."

"What if the kid's with him?"

"Tell him to take a walk, the grown-ups gotta talk."

"How hard you want me to go?"

"Hard enough he stops asking tough questions."

25

Benny Slick's heart nearly stopped. Mario Payday was calling on him *again*? The elderly bookie had survived one meeting with Mario Payday, a small miracle in itself, seeing as how Benny had no visible assets, but he had no chance of surviving a second. If the marker he had produced didn't hold up — and clearly it hadn't or Mario wouldn't be back — then Benny was history, and a pretty sordid one at that. The next twenty minutes were not going to be worth living. The only question was how many of them would involve hanging upside down out the open window.

Probably not many. To the best of Benny's recollection, no one had ever been pulled up twice. You were lucky to find an answer that got you pulled up once. The second time out the window was a one-way trip guaranteed. There was no escape. If the window had been open, Benny might have gone out it himself.

"Ah, Mr. Slick," Mario said. "I had not expected to be seeing you so soon."

Benny tried to answer. It came out a strangled whine, eerily close to the pitch of a hospital monitor flatlining.

Mario Payday nodded approvingly. "Well said." He grabbed the back of the chair Benny had just vacated, spun it around, and sat down. "I believe you've met my boys, Carlo and Ollie the Ox."

Ollie looked like an ox. One that had just been slammed in the forehead with a sledge-hammer at the slaughterhouse. His eyes registered no discernible intellect whatsoever.

"Now then, with regard to your marker, or rather Mr. Fisher's marker, the one that you gave me in an attempt to resolve your outstanding debt."

Benny swallowed hard. He was surprised to discover he still had saliva. He did not trust himself to speak.

"I brought up the matter with Mr. Fisher, who was most surprised to see me. He expressed the opinion that the debt had been paid, and that you surely knew it had."

Benny found his voice. "That's not true, he's lying — of course he'd say that, what else was he going to say? You think he wants to give you ninety thousand dollars, of course he doesn't, he's trying to get out of it. I can't believe you'd fall for that."

Benny suddenly realized he'd said the word *fall*. His head automatically swiveled toward the window, as if propelled by an irresistible force. He looked back, but it was too late. Mario had followed his gaze.

"What a charming idea," Mario said. "Carlo, could you help Mr. Slick recover his composure? I think I know just where to look."

Benny's eyes were wide. He opened his mouth to protest but nothing came out. No agonized wail, no stammered excuse, no halfhearted plea for mercy when there was none to be had. He simply stopped. His face froze, and he blinked twice and pitched forward onto his face.

"Oh, for goodness sakes," Mario said. "Why must they be so dramatic? Carlo, get him up. Dust him off. We've wasted more than enough time on this gentleman. His excuse isn't going to fly. But *he* is." Mario chuckled. "That's rather clever. I hope he heard me. Get him up and ask him."

Carlo rolled Benny over and slapped him in the face. Benny didn't respond. Carlo put his head on his chest and listened for a heartbeat. He found none.

Carlo looked up. "I think he's dead."
Mario flicked cigar ash off his pants leg.
"Well," he said, "that's inconvenient."

26

By the time the whole Tommy Taperelli question got sorted out, it was lunchtime and the court broke for lunch. The upshot was that Herbie could ask the question, but if the witness denied the allegation, that would be that. There would be no follow-up. It seemed fairly straightforward, still it took forever to agree upon. And when, surprise, surprise, Detective Kelly answered that his testimony had not been influenced in the least by Tommy Taperelli, Herbie's bombshell was, in the final analysis, a bit of a dud.

Herbie was somewhat preoccupied on his way to lunch. He stepped off the curb and was almost run over. He jumped back and was surprised to have the car stop right alongside him. The door flew open and two goons pulled him into the backseat.

After the morning in court Herbie fully expected it to be Tommy Taperelli's henchmen about to take him for a ride. In which case, a beating would be a benign outcome.

He was not prepared for the smiling face of Mario Payday.

"Mr. Fisher, how nice of you to drop by."

"Thanks for the invitation."

"But of course. When a man of your stature comes to my attention, I would not want him to feel slighted."

"That wasn't a worry."

"I'm glad. Anyway, you seemed so certain there was something wrong with your marker, I asked Benny Slick to clarify the situation."

"What did he say?"

"Unfortunately, the gentleman was no longer able to answer the question. Or any other, for that matter."

"You didn't!"

"Of course not, Mr. Fisher. He was an old man. He had a heart attack."

"While hanging upside down?"

Mario smiled and waggled his finger. "Good one, Mr. Fisher. I like your sense of humor. If only it was rivaled by your sense of obligation. I am wondering if you have made any progress toward bringing our business transaction to a satisfactory conclusion."

"I've been somewhat busy."

"So I understand. A lawyer appearing in court would have to be a very busy man. Particularly in a criminal case, and especially when his client is the son of a prominent man. A lawyer would have to work very hard in order to justify his retainer."

"I see you have an intimate knowledge of the law."

"I consulted a lawyer once. He wanted *me* to pay *him*. A novel idea. It took some time to set him straight."

"Mr. Capelleti —"

"Mario. Please."

"Mario, I hate to disappoint you, but I've been having a hell of a day. If you want to beat me up, you'll have to get in line."

"Beat you up? Heaven forbid. We're gentlemen, you and I. And we will settle this like gentlemen."

"You're proposing a duel?"

Mario smiled. "What a novel idea. I like you, Mr. Fisher. I really do. I am delighted that fate has thrust us together."

"It's a blessing," Herbie said. "Well, I'm glad we had this little chat."

"As am I, Mr. Fisher. It's not only pleasant, but it gives me an opportunity to remind you of your obligation to me, which I expect you to discharge."

Mario signaled to the driver and the car

124

pulled up to the curb. Carlo came around and opened the door. Before Herbie could get out, Mario put a hand on his arm.

"In cash, by the end of the business day. Is that clear, Mr. Fisher?"

Herbie smiled. "Crystal."

27

The afternoon session was a wash. Herbie managed to jolt the detective a few times, and made a good case for the fact that he was in a perfect position to frame the defendant, but the jurors weren't impressed, and as testimony wore on he got the impression many of them weren't even listening.

He also managed to rack up two contempt of court citations and fifteen hundred dollars in fines, in each case for persisting in a line of questioning the judge had ruled inadmissible. At least those instances seemed to arouse the interest of the jury.

By the time court adjourned Herbie was happy just to get out of there.

Councilman Ross came down the aisle and stopped him. "Is any of that true?"

"Is any of what true?"

"The detective is framing my son?"

"I think there's a good chance."

"You've got to prove it."

"That's a problem."

"Why? Lawyers get clients off by claiming police corruption all the time."

"Sure. Because it isn't true. It's just a smokescreen and people buy it. This is different. I think your son's telling the truth, and in this case it actually happened. Detective Kelly knows all the facts, and he'll just keep covering up."

"I need to talk to you."

"You are."

"Not here." The councilman said, "David," in a preemptive fashion, turned on his heel, and walked out of the courtroom.

Herbie looked at his client. David seemed embarrassed, probably that he was going to go along.

Herbie followed David outside, where the councilman had a limo waiting.

"Hmm. Man of the people," Herbie said.

David sniggered. He was used to people kowtowing to his father. Someone standing up to him was a refreshing change.

The limo whisked them up to the councilman's Fifth Avenue address. They went inside and up in the elevator.

Councilman Ross's foyer seemed unnecessarily opulent to Herbie. "If you're trying to impress me, I happen to know Stone Barrington."

127

"Well-to-do, is he?"

"His town house rivals this, plus he has half a dozen houses including an English country manor, not to mention the chain of Arrington hotels he's opened around the world. He also owns and flies his own jets."

"Good for him."

Ross ushered them into a sitting room slightly smaller than Madison Square Garden. "All right. What's your next move?"

"I have no idea. Actually, I was hoping you could help me out."

"What do you mean?"

"Why is this happening?"

Ross frowned. "I don't understand."

"Someone is framing your son. Why? That's what I can't figure. Usually, with a drug bust of this kind, someone is framed because they can't get him legitimately and they want to get him off the street, or they frame him to take the heat off somebody else. Neither of those scenarios makes any sense. But, his father's a councilman. So, have there been any unusual demands on you lately?"

"There are always demands on me."

"That's not helpful. Do you happen to know Tommy Taperelli?"

"I've heard of him, of course. I've never met him."

"How about Jules Kenworth?"

Councilman Ross blinked. "Why?"

"He's in bed with Taperelli and Taperelli's in bed with Kelly. You do the math."

"I see."

"You know Kenworth, don't you?"

"I've had some dealings with Jules Kenworth."

"And?"

"He's a crook. Always looking to cut a corner."

"Did he ask you to cut one?"

"No. But he's always trying to line up votes for his projects."

"Like what?"

"Building ordinances he wants lifted, to get around restrictions."

"Did you ever vote for him?"

"Not that I recall."

"I would think you'd recall."

"No, I've never voted for one of his petitions. Or if I have, it's because he was one of many bringing the suit, and it wasn't just to benefit him."

"What about lately?"

"I know I've turned everything down. I don't want to be associated with that man."

"Would he frame your son?"

"I can't believe he'd do that."

"Why not? You don't like him."

"What would he gain?"

"You tell me."

Herbie's cell phone rang. He didn't want to answer it. There were so many people he didn't want to talk to. He pulled it out and checked caller ID. Melanie Porter. Herbie didn't know any Melanie Porter. He expected it to be a secretary at Woodman & Weld.

Herbie clicked it on. "Hello?"

"Herbie Fisher?"

"Yes."

"Melanie Porter."

"Yes."

"I want to talk to you about the case."

"Oh?"

"Are you where you can't talk?"

"At the moment I'm in a meeting with Councilman Ross."

"Oh, for goodness sakes. Is he giving you any straight answers?"

"That's a matter of opinion."

"I'm sure he isn't. Daddy will never learn."

"Who?"

"Oh, for goodness sakes. This always happens. The name threw you. I'm the councilman's daughter. Daddy's sweet, but he's a politician."

"Uh-huh."

"You're never going to get anywhere talking to him. Make an excuse to get out of there and call me back."

The phone clicked dead. Herbie slipped it back in his pocket and found David and the councilman looking at him.

He grimaced. "I'm sorry. Something came up. I have to go, but that's okay because you don't need me for this conversation. I can't help you right now. Only you can help you. You need to jog your memories, come up with some reason why this is happening. If Kenworth's involved, why would he want to frame your son? Assuming that has anything to do with anything and it's not just a monstrous coincidence. Just because the detective's dirty doesn't mean that's what this is all about. Leaving your father out of it, is there anyone out to get you for your own sake? A disgruntled ex-girlfriend, for instance, who just wants to watch you squirm?"

"Not at all."

"If that's a ridiculous notion, rule it out. We need to get ahead of this thing because if your son is innocent, someone's gone to an awful lot of trouble to make him look like he isn't. If you come up with anything, give me a call."

Herbie turned on his heel and walked out.

131

28

While the doorman hailed him a cab, Herbie whipped out his cell phone and called Melanie back.

"Where are you?" she said.

"Hailing a cab."

"Meet me on the corner of Broadway and a hundred and tenth."

"How will I know you?"

"I'll be the one who walks up to you and says, 'Herb Fisher?'"

"How do you know me?"

"I Googled you. I trust you still look like the geek in the Woodman & Weld photo."

"I wouldn't count on it," Herbie said. "They Photoshopped out my handlebar mustache and muttonchops."

Herbie got out of the cab at 110th and Broadway and looked around for Melanie.

A hand tapped him on the shoulder.

Herbie turned around to find a beautiful woman smiling at him. Her blond hair was tucked back in a tidy chignon, lending maturity to a face that looked younger than her years. Herbie wasn't sure what her years actually were, he just knew she was older than David. Otherwise, he could have taken her for a freshman.

"Well, well," she said, "if it isn't my kid brother's attorney. Come on, I'll buy you a drink."

"Are you always this brusque?" Herbie said.

"Only when my brother's facing jail time. Come on, there's a little bar up the street."

She took him up Broadway to a funky college bar. It was a little loud for Herbie's taste, but his college days were in the rearview mirror. They were lucky enough to get a table for two along the wall.

"So," Melanie said, "the advantage of this place is we can talk without being overheard."

"Or hearing each other."

"Hard of hearing, Gramps? I can lean close and shout. So, is my father any help?"

"In a word, no."

She shook her head, deploringly but fondly. "Always the politician. You tried to connect the detective to Tommy Taperelli, didn't you?"

"How do you know that?"

133

"I have a reporter friend who covers the crime beat."

"Sits in on court cases?"

"Yeah."

"Why would he sit in on this one?"

"Because it's my brother."

"Ex-boyfriend?"

"Why do you say ex?"

"If he was your boyfriend, he'd be here."

Melanie smiled. "You're very quick. I suppose that's an advantage in a lawyer. I always thought of them as stodgy and doddering."

"Not the lawyers on TV."

"No, but on TV no one's stodgy and doddering. Even stodgy and doddering people aren't."

"I take it you're not a lawyer."

Melanie shook her head. "No. I'm a doctor. I was premed at Columbia. Now I'm an intern at Cornell Hospital."

Herbie liked her. There was an ease about her that made him feel relaxed for the first time all day, and it had been a hell of a day. He found himself actually smiling as the conversation progressed.

"So what information did you want to share with me?" Herbie said.

"Yeah. About Tommy Taperelli. Can you really link the detective to him?"

"I have it on good authority."

"How good?"

"You wouldn't believe."

"Try me."

"I can't give up my source."

"That's reporters, not lawyers."

"I'm friends with the commissioner of police."

Melanie's mouth fell open. "The police commissioner says the detective is tied to Taperelli?"

"Did I say that? I don't recall saying that."

"Never mind sparring with me. If they're actually connected, there's your link. Tommy Taperelli is in bed with Jules Kenworth."

"So I understand."

"My father told you?"

"Your father says Kenworth is a crook and he wouldn't deal with him."

"That's the short version. Before he got into politics my father had dealings with Kenworth. When he found out they were illegal, he got out."

"So?"

"Kenworth never lets you get out. He's always after my father to do something for him."

"Just to be a prick?"

"No, there's lots of money involved. The

city council rules on construction ordinances. Kenworth will want my father to vote his way on some project or other. My father always turns him down."

"How come?"

"There's always a reason. Just the fact that he's asking means he's trying to bend the rules. And it's always something you wouldn't want to be associated with."

"What do you mean?"

"Oh, like there's a museum or a library with landmark status he wants to get lifted so he can knock it down and build something. It's a poison pill. If my father ever voted for one, he could forget about reelection. There's no way he'd go along with one of Kenworth's schemes."

"Even with your brother facing a jail sentence?"

"Perhaps. But I think my father half believes David's drug arrest was legitimate."

"I think David is innocent."

"You're his lawyer. You have to think that."

"No, I don't. If he were guilty, I'd strongly encourage him to take the plea."

"What if he wouldn't?"

"Then he could get another lawyer."

"That's not how lawyers work."

"Well, I'm not a criminal attorney. I haven't learned the rules yet."

Melanie peered at his face. "Your eyes are twinkling. Are you kidding me?"

"I've had a long day."

They smiled at each other.

Herbie's cell phone rang. He jerked it out, clicked it on. "Hello?"

It was Yvette. "Hi, honey. When are you coming home?"

Herbie found himself suddenly embarrassed to be talking to Yvette in front of Melanie. "I got held up with work," he said.

"Life of a lawyer! If you can, get home soon. I'd like to give you a proper kiss good night," she said suggestively.

"I'm wrapping things up here and should be there soon."

Herbie clicked the phone off to find Melanie smiling at him. "I take it you need to go?"

"Not enough hours in the day. Sorry to cut this short."

"Me too. Walk me home, it's only two blocks."

They settled the check and Herbie walked her to a brownstone on 114th Street.

"This is me," she said.

Herbie felt awkward about saying good night. A handshake? That didn't seem right. What should he do?

While he was hesitating, Melanie took his

face in her hands, said, "Save my brother," and kissed him lightly on the lips.

Before Herbie could say anything, she disappeared in the front door.

On the other side of the street, Mookie whipped out his notebook and scribbled down the address.

29

As they lay together after a satisfying tumble in bed, Yvette was concerned. Herbie had felt distant, preoccupied, and he was lacking his normal level of enthusiasm.

"Are you okay? You seem a little distracted."

"Tough day in court."

"Where'd you go after?"

"My client's father wanted to talk to me. Which was a switch. First he wanted to fire me."

"Aw, who would want to fire you?"

"Anyone with any sense," Herbie said.

He was uncomfortable with the conversation because he wasn't mentioning Melanie. There was no reason not to, still, he didn't feel like bringing her up. It was one of those situations. Awkward for no good reason.

"You want me to make you a drink?" Yvette said.

"Sure."

Yvette hopped naked from the bed and flounced over to the bar in the den. She frowned as she mixed the drinks. Was he on to her? Was Donnie right about giving her name to the cops? Had they run her record and told Herbie? His friend was a cop. His friend was the *top* cop. And he had been there, supervising the whole thing. If they had run her record, they'd have told him about her past. And he'd have told Herbie, and Herbie would know, and that would be why he was acting so funny just now, not at all like himself. Preoccupied, and guarded, like he was keeping something from her. And what could that be except that he knew who she was?

Well, too late now. The gig was either blown or it wasn't. Nothing to do but go ahead as if it wasn't. Play the part and hope for the best.

Damn it, Donnie was right. Yvette hated it when Donnie was right. Which, she conceded, was more often than not.

He was right, but he was reckless. He could blow the gig on his own and still be right, just chalk it up to bad luck. But if she blew it, there'd be hell to pay. He'd give new meaning to the words *revenge sex*. She'd be lucky if she was able to walk.

Yvette steeled herself, slapped a smile on her face, picked up the martinis, and headed back to the bedroom.

30

Taperelli picked up the phone. "Yeah?"

Mookie wasn't happy. "There's no James Glick in any goddamned hospital in the whole goddamned city."

"Are you sure?"

"I called every fucking one," Mookie said, "and believe me, it wasn't easy. A lot of them got switchboard systems, you know, 'If you're a doctor trying to reach another doctor and you think you're mighty fucking important, press one. If this is an emergency, hang up and call nine-one-one, because by the time you get through to us you'll be dead.' "

"Yeah, yeah," Taperelli cut in. "But you got through?"

"Sure. I pretended to be a doctor until I got a human being, then I asked for admitting. Worked every time. And James Glick isn't there. He isn't in any hospital in the suburbs, either, and why should he be, we have his address and he lives in Manhattan, but I checked 'em anyway because I knew you'd ask. James Glick is playing a game with us."

"Go to his apartment. If he doesn't answer, break in. If he's there, bring him here. If he's gone, find out where."

"That's a relief."

"What?"

"To get off the damn phone."

James Glick lived in a four-story brownstone that had been divided up into apartments. His apartment was 2B. Mookie rang the downstairs bell, but no one buzzed the door. He started ringing doorbells at random until someone buzzed him in. A woman in a first-floor apartment pushed her door open, saw Mookie heading for the stairs. "You buzz me?"

"Hell, no."

Mookie went up the stairs to apartments 2A and 2B. He'd been careful not to buzz 2A. He didn't want that door opening while he was letting himself into James Glick's apartment.

Mookie's methods were not subtle. He took a crowbar out from under his coat, inserted it into the doorjamb, and pried back. Wood splintered and metal flew as the door popped open.

It didn't take Mookie long to determine that James Glick was gone. His toothbrush and razor were missing from the bathroom, and one of his dresser drawers was left open.

Mookie looked around for something that would give him a clue where Glick had gone. The guy had a computer on his desk. Mookie clicked the mouse, found that it had been left on. Mookie checked his e-mail. The last e-mail was a confirmation of an Amtrak ticket. James Glick had taken the Acela to Washington, D.C.

Mookie jerked the cell phone out of his pocket. "Bad news, boss."

"What's that?"

"James Glick skipped town."

31

Dino called Stone. "Are you up for dinner?"

"Sure. I gather Viv is on a job and unfree to entertain you?"

"Viv's always working, but in this case I have news," Dino said. "Patroon at seven?"

"Have they repaired the damage?"

"Does it matter? It's just a couple of bullet holes."

Stone arrived first and took the seat with his back to the wall, facing the door.

Dino walked in and chuckled. "Hello, gunslinger. Did you order yet?"

"Just got here."

Dino pulled up a chair and sat down.

"You're sitting with your back to the door," Stone said.

Dino shrugged. "Sure. My buddy's watching the entrance for me."

The waitress came over and took their orders. Dino had the rib eye. Stone ordered the osso buco.

"Something on your mind?" Stone said.

"More bad news."

"Seems to be the only kind you get. What's up?"

"James Glick isn't getting out of the hospital."

"He died?"

"He was never there. James Glick skipped town. I don't know what kind of pressure he was under, but he's taken to flight."

"How do you know?"

"I'm the commissioner of police, I had the hospitals checked. He's not there and never was. He took the Amtrak to Washington, D.C., a couple of days ago. He bought a train ticket to Miami at Union Station, but it's a good bet he never used it because he bought another train ticket from Washington to St. Louis a good two hours after his train to Miami would have left."

"Did he go to St. Louis?"

"If he didn't, someone else stayed over at the Hyatt on his credit card. So James Glick is either on the run, or someone has his wallet. If he's on the run, he's not doing a very good job of it because if I can trace him that easily, others can, too."

"Will you tell Herbie?"

Dino grimaced. "I don't want this to become a bad habit, but what good will telling Herbie do? He knows the guy's not coming back. There's nothing he'd be doing any differently now if he had the information."

"So what are you going to do about Glick?"

"I'll track him, and if there seems any point, I'll pull him in."

"You can do that?"

"With a phone call. We're not the only police department in the country, you know. Though right now, it would only muddy the waters. And they're murky enough as it is."

32

Jules Kenworth had a busy day. A photo op with the mayor, lunch with his trophy wife, a business meeting with an entrepreneur who was lucky to get it. And then some goddamned group he was supposed to be nice to because they were naming a statue after him, as if that really mattered; if they wanted to use his name *they* should be nice to *him.*

Kenworth was pissed off and didn't know why. It was just on general principles. What was the use of having billions of dollars if you couldn't arrange everything to your liking?

The phone rang.

It was Taperelli. If he had bad news, Kenworth was going to tear him a new one.

"Skipped town?" Kenworth thundered. "When the hell did that happen?"

"The day he sent the other lawyer."

"And you're just finding out now?"

"He said he was in the hospital. There was no reason to doubt it until he didn't come out of the hospital."

"So this asshole handling the case is it? You're telling me we're stuck with him?"

"It appears so."

"Then he has to learn, doesn't he?"

"He certainly does."

"Think you can handle that?" Kenworth said.

"Consider it done."

33

Alonzo's meat cleaver froze in mid-chop. He blinked at the man coming in the door and wished he were somewhere else.

"It's Payday!" Mario announced, and Alonzo trembled.

"Take care of your customers, Alonzo, take care of your customers. Do not let me disturb you."

There were three customers in the butcher shop. Carlo put the CLOSED sign on the door to be sure there wouldn't be any more. One of the three customers read the situation right and left without buying anything. The woman awaiting her lamb chops would have done so, too, had she not been in mid-purchase.

Alonzo swung the cleaver, made the chops. They weren't anything close to even, but no one cared. The woman grabbed them gratefully, flung money on the counter, and fled.

The last customer, finally recognizing the

situation, decided there was something he would rather do. He beat a dignified, albeit hasty, retreat.

Carlo locked the door behind him and pulled down the blind.

Mario lit a cigar. "Alonzo. You don't look happy to see me. It's payday. Don't you have the cash?"

"I got the vig."

"Hear that, Carlo? He's got the vig. But there's principal involved. Wouldn't you like to pay it down?"

"I'll have it Thursday."

Mario looked shocked and offended. He spread his arms and shook his head deploringly at the butcher's faux pas. "You're asking me to come all the way back here on Thursday because you are not prepared? That is a serious breach of etiquette. And how do we deal with serious breaches of etiquette, Carlo?"

Carlo looked like an unprepared student who had been called on by the teacher. "Real well?" he guessed.

Mario chuckled and shook his head ruefully. "Well, that's certainly true. But how do we deal with a *person* who has made a serious breach of etiquette?"

"We remind him?"

"Exactly. We remind him. We point out

the error of his ways. Which is what we need to do in this case." Mario smiled at the wretched butcher. "That's a real dangerous profession you have, chopping meat. How many fingers do you have left?"

Alonzo trembled and tried to hide his hands.

Mario said sweetly, "Could Carlo borrow your cleaver?"

The sun was shining brightly as Mario and his goons came out of the butcher shop.

"Who's next?" Carlo said. Carlo felt exhilarated, as he always did after chopping off a finger.

Mario consulted his notebook. "Ah. Herbie Fisher."

"Who?"

"The guy who didn't want to pay."

"They all don't want to pay."

"Idiot. The lawyer you hung out the window."

"A lawyer. What do you do with a lawyer? Hit him with a gavel?"

"That's very funny. You know why you find that very funny? Because he is not holding your ninety grand."

"That's a lot of money."

"Yes, it is. That's not like a few hundred dollars to a butcher. That is serious cash. It requires a serious reminder."

"You want me to shoot at him again?"

"Ah, Carlo," Mario said. He shook his head deploringly, but almost fondly. "Try to learn something. If you hit him, he can't pay. If you miss him, he knows you don't *mean* to hit him. What's the good of that?"

"I could shoot his girlfriend."

Mario blinked. "He has a girlfriend?"

"Yeah. She was with him in the restaurant. They looked like they're in love."

"You might have mentioned this before."

"Why?"

"It's called leverage, Carlo." Mario blew a smoke ring. "So. That's excellent. I gave him twenty-four hours to pay, and he has not done so. I can't let someone stiff me on a debt of that size. It makes me look weak. A man in my profession can't afford to look weak."

"What do you want me to do?"

"We are going to set him up, Carlo. We are going to make him wish he'd paid."

34

Yvette came out the front door of Herbie's apartment building. She smiled at the doorman and declined his offer to get her a cab. Instead, she strolled in the sunshine down Park Avenue. As she was passing the side street, hands grabbed her and pulled her aside.

"Donnie!" Yvette hissed. "What are you doing? You can't be here. Why are you here?"

"Why do you think?"

"I can't keep giving you money."

"Of course not. I wouldn't want you to."

"Really?"

"That would be stupid."

Yvette looked at him suspiciously. "Really?"

"Of course not. Blow our chances just for a few bucks? What a bad move." Donnie stretched and cocked his head. "Though I could use some cash."

"Donnie."

"Relax, I'm not taking your money. Of course, I wouldn't mind taking his."

"Damn it, Donnie."

"Take it easy. Did I say I was doing it? No. I said I wouldn't mind. There's the problem. You've got this wonderful setup, but it's taking a little long, and what am I gonna do for money?"

"You ever think of working?"

"You are funny. So, I was thinking, 'cause that's what I do, 'cause one of us has to, so I was thinking, how can I take some of this guy's money without taking his money."

"Oh, you were thinking that? There's a brilliant idea."

"Actually, it is. See, this guy's rich. He's got all this expensive shit."

"I am not stealing from him."

"Of course not. *I* am. All you have to do is what you've been doing. And you do it so well, don't you, honey?"

"What are you talking about?"

"Don't worry, I've got it all worked out." Donnie handed her a little glass vial. He put it in her palm, wrapped her fingers around it. "You take this, you put it in his drink. You mix him drinks, don't you, honey? So you mix this one. And he goes to sleep, just for a little while — you're not poisoning him, just a nice, deep sleep. And

155

while he's out, I steal his stuff."

"And how am I going to explain *how his stuff vanished from under my nose*?" Yvette asked sarcastically.

"What's to explain? You're going to show me the stuff he never uses. The stuff he never even looks at. He won't even know he's been robbed."

"Oh, yeah? How are you going to rob him? You can't get in."

He laughed. "Oh, how little you know."

35

Herbie was on his way up Centre Street toward the courthouse when two goons fell into step next to him.

"Aw, come on, guys, give it a rest," Herbie said.

The goons flanked him and took him by the arms.

"I hate to spoil your fun, but I really don't have time to hang upside down for you right now."

No one was paying the least attention to him. The goons marched him down the street to a stretch limo, thrust him inside, and slammed the door.

The man sitting in the backseat was flashily dressed. His clothes were expensive but showed little taste. He looked as if a great deal of care had been taken to make him appear just wrong. The effect was vulgar, while meant to be impressive.

He smiled cordially and said, "Please, sit down."

Herbie sat in the seat facing him.

"Would you care for a drink?"

"Thank you, I have to be in court."

"Yes, I know. You're Herb Fisher." He cocked his head. "Do you know me?"

"I don't believe we've met."

"I'm Tommy Taperelli."

"Ah, yes. The man with no ties to Detective Kelly."

Taperelli smiled. "That's funny. Keep that sense of humor and we'll get along fine. That's right, I'm the man with no ties to Detective Kelly. And since I don't have any, there's no reason to waste time trying to prove I do."

"Is that right?"

"It's not just right, it's essential. This case needs to end today, and not in a plea bargain. In a verdict. Because people need to get on with their lives, for many reasons too numerous to mention. So I thought that's why we should have this talk, one gentleman to another. Because Woodman & Weld is a prestigious firm, but they can't keep running through lawyers like this. It would be a shame if they had to bring in somebody else."

"Let's not let that happen."

"Oh, but it will, if you can't wrap up the case tonight. You either expedite the hearing and the case goes to the jury this afternoon, or your replacement takes a dive tomorrow morning, which would be embarrassing for us both. I don't like to be embarrassed, Mr. Fisher, I like it when things go smoothly." Taperelli smiled. "Are you sure you won't have that drink?"

"I really can't," Herbie said. "But you've certainly given me a lot to think about."

"Oh, don't think, Mr. Fisher. Just do it." Taperelli chuckled.

Herbie smiled at Taperelli. "No problem."

Herbie couldn't help looking around for goons as he walked into court. Mookie, in his usual spot in the back row, seemed a good bet. He wasn't one of the goons who'd dragged him off to Taperelli, still, he had that look. The other goons didn't appear to be there, but that didn't matter, all it took was one to report on what he did or didn't do.

David Ross was bright-eyed and eager at the defense table. He jumped up when Herbie came in. "You're here. I take it James Glick isn't coming."

"I doubt it."

"Good. I won't have to argue with him. I

don't need a lawyer selling me out." David frowned. "What's the matter? You don't look well."

"I'm fine," Herbie said, but it wasn't true. Taperelli's threat was real and immediate. Herbie knew that, just as the reason for James Glick's absence was now readily apparent. The young man wasn't dead — he had spoken to Herbie, very much alive — but the odds of him actually being in the hospital had dropped to zero, and the odds of Herbie winding up there had escalated astronomically.

Herbie was tempted to call a recess and speak to the judge. Unfortunately, Judge Buckingham was not likely to listen. The man was so hostile, Herbie couldn't rule out the idea that he was in bed with Taperelli.

There was no telling where Herbie's actions would leave David Ross. For his first criminal trial, things could not have gone worse. Herbie didn't know much about procedure in such cases. He knew just one thing. He had a duty to protect his client.

At ten o'clock sharp Judge Buckingham called in the jury and returned Detective Kelly to the stand.

"Detective, I remind you that you are still under oath. Mr. Fisher, you may proceed."

Herbie stood up. All he had to do was say, "No further questions." It was not as if there was anything momentous he had to bring out. His bombshell had been Taperelli, and that had fizzled what with the detective's denial and the judge ruling against further questions. The prosecution had other witnesses — the female narc, the lab technician, and the fingerprint expert. Herbie could dismiss Kelly and take his chances with them.

Herbie grimaced.

It wasn't *his* chances.

It was David Ross's.

Herbie stepped up to the witness stand.

He cleared his throat.

"Well, Detective Kelly," he said, "let's go over this again."

Out of the corner of his eye, Herbie could see Mookie get up and go out the back door.

36

Detective Kelly looked very much at ease on the witness stand. He leaned back and regarded the defense attorney with disdain.

Herbie took a breath. "Now, Detective, you said you observed the defendant selling drugs at the party?"

"That's right."

"What exactly did you observe that led you to believe he was selling drugs?"

"A student would come up and talk to him, and they would leave the room together."

"Did you tag along?"

"Of course not. Then he would know we were on to him."

"You were going to bust him anyway. Why would you care if he knew?"

"I didn't want him to suspect before we were sure."

"When did you become sure?"

"The scene I described happened more

than once. When it happened again, he became a more likely suspect."

"But you still weren't sure?"

"Not a hundred percent."

"What percent were you sure?"

"That's an expression, Counselor. You know what it means, and I know what it means, and I'm sure the jurors know what it means, too." Detective Kelly smiled at the jury. One or two of the jurors returned his smile.

"When did you become sure?"

"I would say after the third time we observed the behavior."

"Shortly after?"

"That's right."

"That's interesting, Detective. Shortly after is also an expression. What did you mean by it?"

"I can't give it to you much better than that."

"Well, let's put it this way. You say you moved in shortly after the third time. Was there a fourth time?"

Detective Kelly hesitated.

"You're not sure?"

"I do not have the answers at my fingertips because these are not the questions I expected to be asked."

"What were the questions you expected to

be asked?"

"Objection."

"Sustained."

"If I understand your testimony, Detective, you moved in shortly after the third or fourth time you observed the defendant leave the room with another student."

"That's right."

"And did you arrest the person you believed he was selling to at the time?"

"No, I didn't."

"Why not?"

"We were after the seller, not the buyer."

"And if you wanted to prove sale, wouldn't the best way to do it be to catch the buyer with the packet of cocaine that the defendant had just sold?"

"In a perfect world."

"And this was not a perfect world, Detective?"

"Of course not."

"But was it not a world you created, a world entirely of your own making, a world in which you yourself played a part?"

"So?"

"Why didn't you arrest the buyer?"

"Objection. Already asked and answered."

"It's been asked, but it wasn't answered."

"Overruled."

"Why didn't you arrest the buyer?"

"I explained that."

"No, you have not. Instead, you made some remark about a perfect world."

Herbie was asking questions on automatic pilot. His attention was distracted by the activity in the back of the room. While the detective was testifying, two goons came in, conferred with the goon who'd slipped out, presumably to make a phone call, and returned, and took up positions in the back row on either side of the aisle, effectively blocking the exit.

Clearly Herbie wasn't going to enjoy lunch.

37

Councilman Ross and his son invited Herbie out to lunch with them, but he courteously declined.

"I'm not hungry, and I've got work to do." Herbie smiled. "Hard as it may be to believe, this is not really my case."

Herbie didn't mention the real reason, that if he left the building for lunch there was a strong possibility he wouldn't be back.

After David and his father left, Herbie called Mike Freeman, the head of Strategic Services. Herbie knew Mike well. Aside from setting up the corporate structure of Strategic Defenses, Herbie had often hired Mike's firm to provide security for his clients.

"Hi, Mike. Herb Fisher."

"Herbie. What can I do for you?"

"Funny you should ask. I happen to be appearing in court this afternoon, and I'm going to need a ride home."

"We're not a car service."

"No, but then a limo wouldn't provide the services that I require."

"Oh?"

"There are a couple of gentlemen here who would like to offer me a ride with *them.*"

"Why don't you take it?"

"I don't think we're going in the same direction."

"I see."

"I have every reason to believe there are some people who are not going to be happy with my performance here in court."

"Just how critical *are* these gentlemen?"

"Most likely armed and dangerous and not apt to take no for an answer."

"I have a couple of boys who are very good at saying no."

"I would like to avoid a shooting war. Your boys aren't trigger happy, are they?"

"Not at all. If someone shoots first, that's another story."

"A story I'd rather not star in. I just need a ride home."

"And once you get there?"

"Unless my fiancée tries to kill me, I should be fine."

"You're getting married?"

"I live dangerously."

"So it seems."

Herbie hung up, called a deli down the street and had a sandwich delivered. It had just arrived when the two goons who walked him to the limo came in and conferred with the other goons.

Herbie paid off the delivery boy and headed down the aisle, away from the goons. He pushed through the gate, went up, and sat at the judge's bench.

The bailiff looked horrified. "You can't do that."

"I just did."

"No, no, no. You can't sit there."

"Where can I sit?"

The bailiff pointed to the spectators section. "Out there."

"No, I'm afraid I can't sit there."

"Yes you can, it's perfectly fine."

Herbie smiled. "We're talking at cross purposes. Assume I can't sit here and I can't sit there. Is there a place back there I could hide out?"

"Yes, if you want."

The bailiff led Herbie back to the small conference room where he had first conferred with ADA Grover.

"Will this do?"

"This will be great," Herbie said. He

plunked his sandwich on the table and sat down.

"Okay," the bailiff said. "You can hang out here as long as you want. Is there anything else you need?"

Herbie frowned and considered. "Could you lock me in?"

38

That evening, the Strategic Services car pulled up in front of Herbie's apartment building. There was nothing to distinguish the black sedan from any number of car services, except for the two men in the front seat. Not that they couldn't have passed for limo drivers, but limos didn't have two.

The agent riding shotgun hopped out and came around to open the door for Herbie. He beat out the doorman with a little skip-step, said, "Allow me," and interposed his bulk between the man and the car.

Herbie emerged, amused by the byplay. "Thanks, guys, I think I can take it from here."

"What time tomorrow?" the agent said.

"Nine o'clock, unless you hear different."

Despite the dismissal, the agent watched until Herbie had crossed the lobby and gotten into the elevator, before getting back in the car and driving off.

Carlo almost missed him. He was leaning against a car on the other side of Park Avenue waiting for Herbie to get home. He was alert when the Strategic Services car pulled up in front of the awning, but when a man he didn't recognize emerged, his attention waned. Carlo was just unwrapping another stick of gum and feeding it into his mouth when he caught a glimpse of Herbie going into the building.

That was a close call. Mario would have been pissed.

Carlo whipped out his cell phone and called the office. "He's home."

39

Herbie was distracted. Yvette could tell at once. She tried to get him interested, but he wanted to talk about the trial. Yvette couldn't care less about the trial, but she feigned an interest. It wasn't hard, still it seemed like work.

And underneath it all was the nagging thought that, somehow, Herbie was on to her. That his lack of interest was because he couldn't bear to touch her. Because he was just stringing her along, waiting for her to hang herself.

Yvette knew that wasn't even remotely possible, that it made no sense. It was just that she was doing what Donnie wanted, and doing what Donnie wanted was always risky. It wasn't that Herbie *had* suspicions, it was that she was about to raise them. And it wasn't her fault, damn it, it was all Donnie. And the worry was making her self-conscious and arousing his suspicions.

Herbie flung himself into a chair and shook his head. "I'm sorry. I'm laying all this on you. Bringing my troubles home from work. The worst thing a guy can do. Who would want to marry a guy like that?"

Yvette nearly choked on her reply. Was he setting her up? Of course not. Things were fine. That was the only way to play it, as if things were fine.

She smiled coquettishly. "Would you like me to get your mind off work?"

Herbie relaxed for the first time since he'd been home. "You can do that?"

"Let me make you a drink. Martini?"

"Please."

Donnie signaled to the waitress and ordered another cup of coffee. He didn't need the caffeine, he was jangly enough already, but he couldn't sit in the diner without something in front of him. And he wasn't going to order their seventeen-dollar hamburger. Where the hell did they get off charging seventeen dollars for a burger — they were a diner, for Christ's sake.

Donnie wasn't worried about the job, he liked the job, it was the waiting that got to him. That was the problem with the long con. He didn't have the temperament for it. The payoff was great, but the setup was excruciating. He didn't know why Yvette couldn't understand that. Of course, she was reaping the fruits of the con already, living the life of Riley in a Park Avenue penthouse, and she had the nerve to lecture him on patience.

The waitress brought the coffeepot and hit him with a refill. She didn't write it down, so it was probably free. The waitress had a pad of unpaid orders hanging out of her pocket. His wouldn't be much. He should probably leave her a tip.

There were a couple of blank pads next to the register that Donnie had spotted on his way in. He sipped his coffee and determined that it would be easy to swipe one on his way out. The devil was in the details, and he was determined to get this right.

Yvette shook up the martinis and strained them into chilled glasses. She took out the vial Donnie had given her, emptied it into Herbie's glass, and stirred it around. She wrapped the vial in a tissue and placed it carefully in the bottom of the empty waste-basket behind the bar. Donnie had promised to take it with him. She had to remember to remind him.

Yvette picked up the martinis and had a moment's panic when she couldn't remem-

174

ber which was which. She paused to consider. It was definitely the one closer to the shaker, the one she'd stirred after dropping the liquid in. As she slunk back into the living room, she wondered how long it would take for the drugs to kick in.

40

Carlo and Ollie the Ox cased Herbie's apartment building.

The garage posed no real problem. The entrance, as with all garages in Park Avenue apartment buildings, was on the side street where they were less likely to be noticed. Distracting the lone security guard was the worst of it. A small incendiary device between two parked cars did the trick. The flare went up, the guard went out, and the boys went in.

Carlo located a bunch of circuit breakers, sorted out the wires, and put the camera out of commission, while Ollie stood guard. Standing guard was one of the things Ollie did best, along with breaking heads.

Once the cameras were out of commission, Carlo and Ollie the Ox made their way up the back stairs. Those cameras, Carlo explained, were the least likely for the security guard to notice missing from his screen.

Ollie wasn't impressed. As far as he was concerned, if they were going to the penthouse, they could damn well take the elevator. It took all of Carlo's wiles to talk him down from that position.

With a great deal of grumbling, the two thugs started climbing.

Carlo cursed the piece of pie he'd had for lunch, and tried not to count the floors.

41

Herbie was out like a light, and it wasn't from the lovemaking. Yvette was good, but she wasn't that good. Donnie's stuff had done the trick.

"Herbie?" she said tentatively.

There was no response.

Herbie was out cold.

Yvette picked up the phone and called Donnie.

"Okay," she said.

Donnie was in a quarrelsome mood. "Okay he's out, or okay you gave it to him, or okay you're *going* to give it to him? Give me a little more than that."

"He's out cold. Really cold. Are you sure it wasn't too much?"

"It wasn't too much," Donnie said, and broke the connection.

Donnie hoped it wasn't too much. He'd given Yvette three times the normal dose, just to be sure.

Donnie left a dollar on the counter, paid his check, and swiped the pad. He walked up Lexington Avenue, fished a pizza box out of the garbage can on the corner, and wrote up a takeout order for a large pepperoni pie. He filled in Herbie's name and address, and a twenty-dollar charge for the pizza. It occurred to him there was no reason not to collect the twenty bucks.

There was a lilt in Donnie's step not entirely attributable to caffeine as he made his way over to Park Avenue.

The doorman was out front under the awning.

Donnie sauntered up and said, "Pizza delivery."

"Who's it for?"

"Let me see." Donnie referred to the receipt. "Fisher? Herb Fisher?"

The doorman nodded. "Penthouse."

"Thanks."

"I'll have to call up."

Donnie nodded. "Of course, of course. Classy joint."

Donnie followed him inside, where the doorman called Herbie's apartment on the intercom.

Yvette answered. "Yes?"

"Got a pizza delivery for Mr. Fisher."

"Send him up."

The doorman put down the phone and pointed. "Go on up. Take the elevator to the penthouse."

"Which apartment?" Donnie said.

"It's the whole floor."

Donnie knew that. He just asked so he could express his contempt for the über-wealthy. He rolled his eyes and shook his head. He headed for the elevator, thinking he really should have been an actor.

42

Ollie the Ox reached the top floor. He was pissed, and Carlo was nervous. It was not good to piss off Ollie the Ox.

"Which door?" Ollie said.

"There's only one," Carlo said.

"There's two."

"One is the front door, one is the kitchen door."

"Not hungry," Ollie said. He went to the front door and rang the bell.

Yvette had barely gotten off the phone with the front desk when the doorbell rang. How could Donnie be so fast? The doorman must have sent him up while he was calling. She would have to ask Herbie to speak to him about that. He should wait for approval before sending anyone up.

She flung the door open, stopped, and gasped.

Two goons stood in the doorway. They

181

looked as startled to see her as she was to see them.

The big one just said, "Huh?" but the other one registered recognition.

"Hey, it's her!" Carlo said.

Ollie the Ox said, "Oh." It took a few moments for his brain to wrap itself around the concept. He reached under his coat, pulled out a pistol.

Yvette gawked.

The silencer screwed onto the barrel made it look as long as a blowpipe, so at first she didn't realize what it was. It was only at the last second, before the shot fired, that her face registered fear. Within seconds her eyes rolled back, she sank to the floor, and everything went dark.

43

"Come on, let's get her boyfriend," Carlo said.

"What's he doing?"

"I don't care, as long as he's not calling nine-one-one. Come on. Knock him out and set the scene."

But when the two men walked into the bedroom, they found they didn't have to knock him out. Herbie was stark naked and dead to the world.

"Excellent. Get the girl."

Ollie went out to the foyer and came back with Yvette. "Where do you want her?"

"Other side of the bed."

Ollie flopped her down.

Carlo arranged her on the pillow. "We won't need this," he said. He pulled off the negligee and threw it in the corner. "Okay, here she is, hot to trot, and here's her lover who thinks she's been with another man."

"Why does he think that?"

"Guys do. Okay, here we go." He put the gun in Herbie's hand. "He popped her, and passed out."

Ollie frowned. "He shoots a stark naked girl and goes to sleep?"

Carlo wrapped Herbie's fingers around the gun, pulled the trigger, and fired a shot into the headboard.

"What did you do that for?" Ollie said.

"Framing the guy. That's what this is all about. Come on, let's get out of here."

They went out the front door.

"We got to take the fucking stairs?" Ollie said.

"Down is easy. Come on."

"Aw, fuck!"

They disappeared down the stairwell just as the elevator arrived on the floor.

44

Donnie stepped out of the elevator and found the front door open. He was not surprised. If the guy was unconscious, there was no need to be careful. Nevertheless, he tapped his knuckles on the door frame to make sure the coast was clear.

There was no answer.

What the hell was Yvette doing?

He wandered through the apartment, made his way into the master bedroom, and stopped dead.

Yvette was spread out on the bed stark naked. Red blood ran down the side of her face. It made a stripe across her breast and ended in a small pool on the sheet.

The guy was stark naked, too, and clutching a gun. A murder-suicide? No, he was out, from the knockout drops. How did that compute? He realized he'd been doped and pulled a gun? But Yvette had called him, said the guy was out. Had he come to after that, just long enough to shoot her to death?

The whole thing was all a bad dream. She was dead, and the cops would be coming . . .

He had to get out of there, but he wasn't going to leave empty-handed, not after everything he'd been through.

According to Yvette, Herbie kept his stuff in a walk-in closet opposite the bath.

Donnie poked his head into the master bath, which boasted a large Jacuzzi tub and a glassed shower with multiple sprays, then pushed his way through the double doors to the walk-in closet.

He was greeted by racks of expensive suits. Donnie had no use for suits, even if they weren't hot. He needed things easily fenced for ready cash. Jewelry, that's what Yvette had said. The guy had cuff links worth more than a car, several watches, and some rings.

Donnie had brought a messenger bag. He emptied the jewelry case into it and looked around for more. There was no reason to be circumspect. The long con was gone. What else did the guy have?

Donnie searched the closet. A metal petty cash box looked promising. Inside was a cash envelope, the type the bank issued, full of bills. He reached in, jerked them out.

186

They were hundreds.

Jackpot.

Donnie shoved the money in his pocket and hurried to the front door. He listened before opening it a crack. There was no one there.

Stairs or elevator? What difference did it make? The doorman had seen him already. He'd seen him go in, now he'd see him go out. If they didn't find the body for a while, they'd think it happened after he left. Hell, the pizza was gone, just a couple of crusts in the discarded box. It would look like they'd eaten long before it happened.

Donnie rode down in the elevator, breathing in and out, trying to calm himself.

Come on, method actor, you're a pizza delivery boy. This is a piece of cake. What does a pizza delivery boy do? Oh, yeah. That's right. He sorts his tip money.

Donnie jerked a roll of bills out of his pocket just as the elevator doors opened. He was halfway across the lobby before he noticed they were hundreds. Donnie hunched over, hiding the denominations from the doorman as he pretended to count his tips.

45

When Carlo got back to the office, Mario was going over the account of Martin Kendrick, who had no idea why he was there. Mr. Kendrick was a steady customer who had borrowed small amounts of money over the years, and had always paid it back on time if not sooner. Mario was looking up the instances in which Martin Kendrick had been early with his payments, and giving him credit in each case. This totally baffled Mr. Kendrick, who couldn't help feeling he had done something wrong.

Martin Kendrick had a right to be confused, because he was actually there for no good reason, at least not involving Mario's accounts. He was there solely to provide Mario with an alibi for Yvette's murder. Mario didn't need an alibi, but he always liked to have one. It was kind of like insurance. If he had one, he wouldn't need one.

Carlo barged in and said, "You wanted

me, boss?"

Mario looked up and smiled. "Yes, yes. We're almost done here. Good work, Mr. Kendrick. I need more customers like you. Would you mind waiting outside for a moment? I need to talk to Carlo here."

From his expression, Kendrick expected to be whacked. His hand was shaking as he opened the door.

"So, how did it go?" Mario said.

Carlo shrugged. "Smooth as silk."

"Did he recognize you before you put him out?"

"Didn't have to put him out. Guy was out when we got there."

"Are you sure?"

"Oh, yeah."

"You're sure he wasn't faking?"

"Believe me, he was out. He looked like he'd been drugged. Hell, I thought he was dead."

Mario nodded. "Did you make the phone call?"

"No. I came here."

"Make the phone call." Mario rolled his eyes and jerked his thumb at the corridor. "I'd like to send this guy home before he bores me to death."

Carlo left Mario to wrap up his non-meeting with Martin Kendrick, and went out to make the call. Working pay phones were scarce, but Carlo had scoped one out that afternoon on the corner of Thirty-sixth and Ninth. It was still working, no sure thing for a street phone. Carlo got a dial tone and called 911.

"I'd like to report a domestic disturbance on Park Avenue."

46

The first cops through the door were uni-formed officers responding to a domestic disturbance call. The doorman hadn't heard anything, and no one had complained to him, but he rang the apartment and got no answer, so the cops went up to check it out.

They were surprised to find the door open. The rookie cop was about to barge right in, but his partner stopped him. She was an old-timer and attached to protocol. She rapped loudly on the door, yelling into the apartment, "Police!"

When they were met with silence, she pulled her service weapon and eased through the door sideways, gun up.

Her partner followed, smirking at her for drawing her gun in a Park Avenue pent-house.

He got quite a shock when they reached the bedroom.

Herbie didn't move. He stayed exactly as

Carlo had posed him, breathing shallowly, the gun still in his hand.

Yvette didn't move, either, but she wasn't going to.

That was all the cops needed to see. The naked tableau told the story.

The rookie reached his hand out for the gun.

"Don't touch that!"

He looked at her in surprise. "Why not?"

"It's a crime scene. Don't contaminate it."

"The guy's alive. You gonna let him keep the gun?"

"No, and I'm not going to touch it, either."

She whipped a handkerchief out of her pocket and lifted the gun gently from Herbie's fingers. She set the gun on the dresser, out of Herbie's reach. "Cuff him. I'll call it in."

"Cuff him? He's out cold."

"Okay, I'll cuff him and you call it in."

The rookie made the call. "Got a homicide here. Husband in custody, wife DOA. Domestic disturbance gone bad." He hung up to find his partner smirking at him. "What's so funny?"

"Domestic disturbance gone bad?"

"What's wrong with that?"

"Like a domestic disturbance could be *good.*"

Herbie was barely stirring when the detectives from the crime scene unit arrived. He was in their way, so they let the patrol officers run him in. With little help from their stumbling, incoherent suspect, they dressed him in sweats and running shoes and took him out to the car. They borrowed a gurney from the EMTs so they wouldn't have to carry him.

They took him downtown and booked him for murder, which ordinarily would have earned him a chat with an ADA, but he was still too out of it to be Mirandized. He'd have to sleep it off. So they did what they always do with prisoners in his condition.

They threw him in the drunk tank.

47

Judge Buckingham glowered at the defense table where David Ross sat alone.

"Mr. Ross, where is your attorney?"

"I don't know, Your Honor."

"Did he inform you that he could not be here?"

"No, Your Honor."

"Or that he would be late?"

"No, Your Honor."

"Have you heard from Mr. Fisher this morning?"

"No, I have not."

"Did you ask that another attorney appear in his stead?"

"I didn't know he wouldn't be here, Your Honor."

"That was not my question. Did you ask for another attorney?"

"No, Your Honor."

"How about Mr. Glick?"

"I have not heard from him, either, Your

Honor."

"Have you attempted to call him?"

"No, Your Honor. And in any case, Mr. Fisher has taken over for him. Mr. Glick would not be prepared to resume questioning at this point."

"That's not what I asked, either. It is not your place to assess how this courtroom should be run. That is my business, and I will thank you to remember it."

"Yes, Your Honor."

Judge Buckingham sat up straight on the bench. "This is unacceptable. Herb Fisher knew he was to be here. Herb Fisher is not here. Herb Fisher is in contempt of court. Issue a bench warrant for his arrest, and haul him in here. I expect to see him at two o'clock sharp to show cause why he should not be held in contempt of court."

Judge Buckingham banged the gavel and stalked from the courtroom.

Councilman Ross joined his son at the defense table.

"Any luck?" David said.

Ross shook his head. "I called Woodman & Weld. They haven't heard from him and have no idea where he is."

"What do we do now?"

"Who else would know?" The councilman frowned. "Who was that friend he mentioned the other night? With the mansions and the planes?"

"Stone Barrington."

"That's the one." Ross whipped out his cell phone and called his secretary. "I need a phone number."

Mookie exited the courtroom and pulled out his cell phone, hesitating as his thumb hovered over the green call button. He didn't want to make this call. He figured Taperelli wouldn't be pleased about the news he had to report.

He figured right.

"What do you mean he isn't there?" Taperelli shouted.

"He didn't show up. No one knows where he is. The prosecutor's pissed, and the judge issued some sort of warrant."

"A bench warrant."

"That's the one."

"The lawyer skipped out?"

"Or it's just another stalling tactic. We'll know at two o'clock."

"I don't want to wait till two o'clock."

"I know, but what can we do?"

"The judge really issued a bench warrant?"

"Yeah. There's cops looking for him."

"That's not good."

"No kidding. You can't compete with cops."

"Damn. The guy skipped out. I wonder what happened."

"You talked to him yesterday. Maybe you leaned on him a little hard."

"You're saying it's my fault?"

"Of course not. But you're an intimidating guy. Maybe he got scared."

"It doesn't add up. He shouldn't have run."

"Well, he's not here. The kid's here with no lawyer. So what do you want me to do? I can't lean on him if he's not here."

"He got any close friends?"

"He's got a girlfriend."

"Oh, yeah?"

"I followed her the other night. He met her for drinks, walked her home, kissed her good night."

"Who's the girl?"

"I don't know."

"Find out. Find out who she is, find out where she works. Keep tabs on her till I tell you different. We'll get to him through her."

"You got it."

Mookie left court and headed for the Upper West Side.

48

Stone Barrington was planning a dinner menu. So far it was a dinner for four, but it was for Saturday night and there was still time to add guests. At the moment it was him, a dinner companion to be named later, and Dino and Viv, and he hadn't even asked Dino and Viv yet.

But all that was incidental. What was important was the food. Stone was considering caviar when Joan poked her head in the door. "Do you know a Councilman Ross?"

The name sounded familiar, but not for any reason Stone could put his finger on. "Can't say as I do."

"He says it's about Herbie."

"I'll take it." Stone picked up the phone. "Yes, Councilman, how can I help you?"

"Herb Fisher mentioned you. Said you were great friends."

"We are indeed, and I can give him the

highest reference if you're looking for an attorney."

"He's already my attorney! He's representing my son."

The councilman's name clicked in Stone's mind. "Ah, yes, I do seem to recollect that now that you mention it."

"He didn't show up in court this morning."

"That doesn't sound like Herb."

"It's true, nevertheless. The judge issued a bench warrant, and no one can reach him."

"Thanks, Councilman. I'll take it from here."

Stone got off the phone and called Dino. "Hey, Dino, I just got a call from Councilman Ross, the father of the kid Herbie's representing. Herbie was a no-show in court this morning, and the judge issued a bench warrant."

"What!"

"No one can find him. Can you circumvent the usual missing persons bullshit and see if he's been taken to any emergency room? I have a bad feeling about this."

"Shit. I should never have told him about Taperelli."

"Do you think Taperelli might have done him harm?"

199

"That's what I'm afraid of. I'll call you back."

Half an hour later, Dino was on the line again and said flatly, "He's in the drunk tank."

"What?"

"Charged with murder."

"Are you kidding me?"

"I wish I were. The victim's his fiancée, Yvette."

"What's he saying?"

"Nothing. He's been in and out of consciousness. I had him transferred to a private cell and he's sleeping it off."

"He's drunk?"

"Or drugged. He reeks of liquor. He was found in bed with the victim, naked and holding the murder weapon. Who knows what he's going to say when he wakes up."

"I'm on my way." Stone slammed down the phone. "Joan! Tell Fred to get the car!"

Fred broke all speed records getting downtown. Stone had no problem seeing his client. Dino had paved the way.

Herbie was sitting on the edge of his bunk, groggy and distraught. He looked up at Stone with tear-stained eyes. "They read me my rights. They say I killed Yvette."

Stone calmed Herbie down the best he could and went to hunt up the ADA in

200

charge of the case.

The ADA turned out to be Dierdre Monahan, with whom Stone had a history. She leaned back in her desk chair and cocked her head. "Hi, Stone. What can I do for you?"

Deirdre Monahan and Herbie had a long and bumpy relationship. She'd been the ADA of record in several of his arrests, including the murder of the mobster Carmine Dattila. She'd actually done Herbie a favor in that case, suggesting he claim self-defense. Which was pretty nice of her, considering the patrolman Herbie had kicked in the balls during one of his other arrests happened to be her brother.

"Let's get real here, Monahan. You know and I know Herbie didn't do it."

"I know no such thing. He was found in bed with the victim. He was holding the murder weapon. And, yes, there is gunpowder on his hand, showing he fired the gun. I'd go so far as to call this one a slam dunk."

"This wasn't some casual one-night stand. Herbie was in love with her. They were engaged. Why would he have killed her?"

"Why does anybody kill his girlfriend? Jealousy? Drunk rage? It's not inconceivable."

"It is when the man in question is Herbie.

He wouldn't hurt a fly."

"Tell that to Carmine Dattila."

Stone shot her an impatient look.

Deirdre sighed. "He was drunk, Stone. He could barely stand up."

"He's been drugged. I want a blood test and a Breathalyzer."

"Little late for a Breathalyzer."

"Come on, this is serious. Herbie stood up in open court yesterday and asked a witness if he was being manipulated by Tommy Taperelli. I don't know if you've had any dealings with Mr. Taperelli, but he does not take kindly to insinuations of that manner. Retaliation is not unexpected. I wouldn't put it past him to frame Herbie for murder. That's kind of a tough break for a young attorney trying to do the right thing, particularly when it isn't even his goddamned case to begin with."

"What are you talking about?"

Stone told her the details of David Ross's case, including the suspected connection between Tommy Taperelli and Detective Kelly.

"Detective Kelly, huh?"

"Do you know him?"

"Not personally."

"But you've heard something about him."

"Nothing I care to be quoted on." Monahan frowned. "You really think this is the result of Herbie's interference in Taperelli's business?"

"I know Herbie didn't do it."

"Well, go ahead and bail him out. Dino's already fast-tracked him to be released on his own recognizance."

"Good talking to you."

ADA Monahan smiled. "Anytime, Stone."

49

Dino Bacchetti flashed his ID at the doorman at Herbie's building. He needn't have bothered. The guy recognized him from TV and was all too happy to send him upstairs.

Crime scene techs were processing Herbie's apartment. Photographs had all been taken and evidence was being bagged and labeled. Dino strode around the apartment and assessed the work.

The martini glasses Herbie and Yvette had drunk from were still on the end tables. The rim of one was marked with lipstick — Herbie had clearly drunk from the other glass. Dino pointed them out to the nearest tech. "When you bag those martini glasses, make sure you tag which is which."

The man wasn't going to say anything to the commissioner of police, but clearly wasn't happy being told how to do his job. "Of course. It's standard procedure."

"Just make sure."

Dino proceeded to the bedroom, where he saw the lead on the case, Detective Brogan. He knew the man to be hardworking and by the book, but lacking in creative thinking. The two men shook hands, and Dino turned his attention to the room.

The crime scene unit had tagged a bullet hole in the headboard. The bullet itself had been dug out and bagged for ballistics.

Dino pointed it out to the detective. "Could the bullet have been fired from where the suspect was found?"

"Sure could. Practically a direct line."

"He missed the decedent by three feet."

"That's right."

"While sitting next to her in the bed?"

"Apparently."

"So he either shot her point-blank while she was sitting next to him in bed, killing her instantly, and then fired another shot, missing her by three feet, or he fired a shot, missing her by three feet, and instead of jumping out of bed and running for her life, she sat there looking at him waiting for the coup de grâce."

The detective shrugged. "That's what a defense attorney will say."

"Yeah," Dino replied, clearly unimpressed.

Seeing he had flubbed and eager to score some points with the commissioner, Brogan changed the subject. "There's evidence the victim's body was moved."

"Oh?"

"Drops of blood near the front door. It's possible he shot her there and carried her into bed."

"And arranged her on the pillow, and took another shot at her and missed? Then he got in bed, lay down, and went to sleep?"

"I'm not saying that happened. I'm just saying the blood near the front door indicates the body may have been moved."

"You got samples of that blood?"

"You bet."

"Carry on, Detective," Dino said.

Dino moved on and continued searching the apartment. In the bar he found the evidence of either Yvette or Herbie mixing the drinks. The melted ice from the cocktail shaker was long gone, but the shaker itself was still on the counter. Dino ticked it off as more evidence to be bagged.

In the wastebasket at the end of the bar, a single tissue was crumpled up. It stood out because the wastebasket itself was so clean. Dino fished it out, put it on the bar. He spread the paper with his fingertips.

Inside was a tiny screw-top vial. Inside were a few drops of liquid. He waved at the crime scene tech he'd seen earlier. "Yeah?"

"More evidence to bag."

The man came over and looked.

"This was in the wastebasket."

The man looked pained. "I'd have gotten there, Commissioner. I have to label everything. I can't cherry-pick."

"No one's criticizing. I'm just looking for anything we can expedite."

Dino continued his once-over of the apartment. In the walk-in closet he found the empty cash box and the empty jewelry case.

Dino shook his head. The poor detective was going to think he was really picking on him.

Dino raised his voice. "Detective Brogan? I found something I think you'll want to see."

50

Herbie was still wobbly on his feet, but between them, Fred and Stone were able to muscle him through the door of Stone's Turtle Bay town house.

Joan looked up from her desk as they came in. "Oh, my," she said. "Do I take it we're going to have company?"

"Herbie's going to be staying with us for a while," Stone said. "His apartment's a crime scene, and he wouldn't be comfortable there anyway. You want to help Fred set him up in the guest room? I need to call Dino."

Dino was eager for an update. "You get him out of there?"

"No problem. Well, actually one problem. The ADA is Dierdre Monahan."

"Ouch."

"Indeed."

"How's Herbie?"

"Distraught. He's still pretty out of it. When they read him his rights, it's the first he'd heard that Yvette was dead. He's still not sure he didn't do it."

"You mean he got taken in by the evidence, just like the cops?"

"No, I mean he's so drunk or drugged or whatever he doesn't remember anything. What about the crime scene? Is there anything that *doesn't* point to Herbie?"

"There's some evidence of a robbery. I'm running it down."

"Do that. It would be nice to have something to tell him when he wakes up."

Stone was just getting off the phone with Dino when Joan came downstairs.

"He's out like a light. We gave him a pair of your pajamas and put him to bed. He was out before his head hit the pillow."

"There may be people looking for Herbie. If anyone calls, there's no need to bother him, just take a message."

"Of course," Joan said.

"There's no reason to say where he is."

"Of course not."

"Some of these callers may be official."

"I understand."

"I don't want you to lie to the police."

"What if they ask me where he is?"

"You don't know."

"But I *do* know."

"When we're done here I'm going to have

209

Fred take Herbie to a safe house where he can hide out. Or I might not. I haven't decided yet. You won't know which. So if anybody asks if you know where Herbie is, you can honestly say that you don't."

"What can I tell them?"

"I'm Herbie's attorney. You can always get a message to him through me."

"What if they want to talk to you?"

"Put them on hold and call me."

"In other words, standard procedure. Okay, I got it." Joan started out. "Do you want me to have Fred get the car?"

"No."

51

Mario Payday acted as if the postman had mislaid the mail. "This is most distressing."

"I know," Carlo said.

"He's not at court, and he isn't home."

"No, and he's not in jail. He's been released."

"So what is the point of putting pressure on an individual if the person in question can't be found? Kind of a waste of effort if you ask me."

"There's a bench warrant out for his arrest."

"I thought he *was* arrested."

"That was for murder. This is for failure to appear in court."

"The gentleman has no end of trouble. Which does not mean I intend to stand at the back of the line."

"Trust me, we're on it. The minute he surfaces, he's yours."

"You just can't tell me when that will be.

Well, I suppose it was too much to ask." Mario waggled his cigar, blew a smoke ring. "I'm famished. Let's see how things look after lunch."

52

Judge Buckingham surveyed the gathering in his chambers with displeasure. "The defense attorney has been arrested?" he said incredulously.

"Yes, Your Honor," ADA Grover said. "When the officers attempted to serve the bench warrant, they discovered that Mr. Fisher was already under arrest."

"For murder?"

"That appears to be the case. We're still trying to sort it out, but apparently Mr. Fisher was found with a dead woman and the murder weapon in his hand."

"I hardly think this is the place to get into the merits of that case," Stone Barrington said.

"And who are you again?" Judge Buckingham said.

"Stone Barrington, Your Honor. Attorney for Mr. Fisher, appearing in his stead. I think you can understand why he is unable to be in court this afternoon."

"You are using a murder arrest as an excuse for his failure to appear in court?"

"It beats 'the dog ate my homework.' "

"So where does that leave us?"

"I believe we are entitled to a mistrial, Your Honor."

ADA Grover nearly gagged. "A mistrial? Because the defense attorney killed someone?"

"Well, the defendant can hardly get a fair trial under the circumstances. Jurors are apt to hold Mr. Fisher's arrest against him."

"What do you propose, Mr. Barrington?"

"If Mr. Barrington would care to take over as defense attorney, we would have no objections," ADA Grover said.

"I'm sure you wouldn't, since I'm totally unprepared and know absolutely nothing about the case. But if you adjourn until tomorrow, I suspect Herb will be able to return."

"What are we going to tell the jury?"

Stone considered. "To say the attorney's been arrested would be highly prejudicial. There's no way to continue after that."

"What do you want to tell them?"

"Court's adjourned until tomorrow. What more do they need to know? They'll grumble a bit and go home."

"And what's going to happen tomorrow morning?"

"I'm sure Mr. Fisher's misunderstanding will be straightened out and he'll be back on the case."

"Misunderstanding?" ADA Grover said sarcastically.

Judge Buckingham said, "All right. I'll adjourn court until ten o'clock tomorrow morning, at which time Mr. Fisher better be here. If he's not, he better be in jail. If he's not, he soon will be."

53

Joan stuck her head in the door. "There's a Detective Wallace calling."

"What does he want?"

"Herb Fisher."

"What did you tell him?"

"I told him I'd take a message. That didn't seem to thrill him, so we went through the rest of the dance. Then he asked to speak to you."

"Then I better speak to him. Thanks, Joan." Stone picked up the phone. "Stone Barrington. May I help you?"

"This is Detective Sergeant Wallace of the NYPD. I'm looking for Herb Fisher."

"Well, you've come to the right place. I'm Mr. Fisher's attorney."

"Where is Mr. Fisher?"

"I'm sure I couldn't tell you."

"I have a bench warrant for Mr. Fisher."

"Have you served it?"

"No."

"Then it isn't binding. Come back when you've served it."

"Don't think you can give me the run-around, Mr. Barrington, just because you're friends with the commissioner. Impeding an officer of the law in the course of carrying out his duty is a criminal offense. It carries a jail sentence."

"I'll bear that in mind. If you're done threatening me, I'd like to get back to business. I am rather busy at the moment."

"I'm telling you that I have reason to believe that the object of the bench warrant, Herbert Fisher, is on your premises."

"What is the reason for that belief?"

"Well, he's not in his own apartment."

"Oh? He's not there so he must be here? I'd love to get you on the stand, Sergeant."

Stone hung up and buzzed Joan. "If Detective Sergeant Wallace should call back, I'm not in."

"Got it. And Herbie's up."

"Oh?"

"He's awake, anyway. Sitting up in bed. He's still groggy. Whatever he was on had quite a kick."

"Good."

"Good?"

"Then it's sure to show up in his blood test."

Stone went upstairs to the guest room. Herbie, dressed in Stone's pajamas, was sitting up in bed. He looked up with tear-stained eyes.

"I didn't do it."

"I know."

"You do?"

"Of course I do. No one thinks you did it."

"The police do."

"I strongly suspect they'll come around to my view."

"This is all my fault."

"No, it isn't."

"Yes, it is. I was stupid and arrogant. I provoked a mob boss in open court."

"You don't know that's why this happened."

"Oh? What do *you* think? I accused a detective of being dirty. The detective *is* dirty. You think he takes that lying down? You think Taperelli doesn't seek revenge? And I didn't even warn Yvette. I didn't say, hey, I'm treading on dangerous ground in court, we have to be careful, we have to look out. I just assumed everything would be fine." Herbie shuddered, shook his head. "Oh, God. I don't know how you come back from something like this."

"I know," Stone said gently.

Herbie looked at him. "That's right. You've been through it with Arrington. How'd you cope? How did you get through it?"

The love of Stone's life and the mother of his son had been killed shortly after they had been reunited and finally gotten married.

"It was hard. But I had to be strong for my son."

"Right. For Peter. You had to be strong for him."

"Yes," Stone said. He didn't know what to say next. Herbie didn't have anyone like that. Herbie didn't have anyone at all, just his work.

"Oh shit, the case! I'm supposed to be in court today!" Herbie lunged unsteadily out of bed.

Stone caught Herbie as he nearly fell, shoving him back onto the bed. "It's all right. I got an adjournment."

"The judge never gave *me* one."

"No. It took something dramatic."

"What did they tell the jury?"

"Nothing. That doesn't mean they won't hear."

"And I'm supposed to stand up in court tomorrow morning as if nothing was wrong?"

"Unless you want to duck out. The judge issued a bench warrant. You'd be fleeing the jurisdiction of the court."

"Big deal. I'm already accused of murder."

"The charge won't stick. Dino's working on it now."

"Personally?"

"He feels bad. He wants to help."

"Nothing helps."

"I know."

Stone's cell phone rang on his way downstairs. He tugged it out of his pocket. "Hello?"

"Stone Barrington?"

"Yes."

"You're Herb Fisher's lawyer?"

"Yes, I am."

"He's really accused of murder?"

"Excuse me. Who are you?"

"Oh. I'm Melanie Porter. David's sister."

"David?"

"David Ross. Herb's his lawyer. What happened?"

"I can't tell you."

"You don't know?"

"You're an anonymous voice on the phone. You could be a clever reporter, for all I know."

"Let me speak to Herb."

"I don't know where he is."

"You don't know where he is?"

"No, but if I hear from him, I'll pass along the message."

Stone clicked the phone off and went back up to Herbie.

"You know a Melanie Porter?"

Herbie reacted to the name. Stone couldn't put his finger on the emotion, but it was a clear response.

"What about her?"

"You know her?"

"Barely. She's my client's sister."

"She called me, looking for you."

"What did you tell her?"

"Nothing. I wanted to check with you to make sure she's legit, not some reporter or cop trying to ferret you out. No one knows you're staying here. You're ducking a warrant, if you'll recall."

"She's fine. Tell her whatever you want."

"She seemed concerned."

"So am I."

Stone went back down and sat at his desk, thinking. He'd managed to put his finger on Herbie's reaction. Embarrassment. Then guilt. He liked the girl. The thought of her flustered him.

Stone took out his cell phone and called Melanie Porter back. "Hello, Melanie? I managed to locate Herb Fisher. Would you like to see him?"

54

Tommy Taperelli's secretary knocked on the door. "Detective Kelly's here to see you."

Taperelli frowned. "Are you kidding me?"

"No, sir. He doesn't have an appointment, but he's most insistent."

"Is there anyone else in the outer office?"

"No."

"Good. Show him in."

Taperelli scowled as Kelly came in. "You've got a lot of nerve coming here. A lawyer stood up in court and accused you of being on my payroll. It's not the brightest time to pay me a call."

"You expect me to just sit there and take it?"

"I expect you to respect the conventions. You don't call on me, I don't call on you. No one puts anyone's job in jeopardy. You want to end your career in a police corruption scandal? Kind of a cushy job to be throwing out the window. Of course, some of those minimum security prisons are quite nice. I'm sure you'll be very comfortable."

"No one saw me come in."

"That you know of. With that asshole lawyer making allegations in court, who knows who might be lurking around. A cop, or maybe a pain-in-the-ass reporter, which would almost be worse, some investigative journalist trying to make a name for himself. They'll stick to you like glue."

"I'm a cop, I know when I'm being watched. No one saw me."

"What's so all-fired important you had to see me in person?"

"I could use a little help. I'm on the witness stand all alone with people sniping at me. I'm giving all the right answers, but the questions are getting harder, and they're asking about you. The judge knocked that down, but it doesn't matter, it means they're on the right track. It's a little late to do something, but, lo and behold, the kid's lawyer disappears. The lawyer simply doesn't show up. The judge issues a bench warrant, and the lawyer *still* doesn't show up."

"So?"

"Did you kill the lawyer?"

"Oh, for Christ's sake!"

"Did you?"

"No, I didn't kill the fucking lawyer. Jesus Christ, if I *did* kill the lawyer, would you want to know?"

"No."

"But you're here asking."

"I gotta know how deep the shit is I'm getting in."

"I had nothing to do with the lawyer disappearing."

"Yeah, well, I'm still on the stand. Now they'll be asking about that."

"It's got nothing to do with you."

"Oh, like that's going to satisfy them."

"It's got nothing to do with me. I don't know what happened, but it wasn't us."

"Of course not."

"I mean it. I had nothing to do with it, I know nothing about it. The same goes for you. You answer the questions that way, no one can touch you. Now get out of here before someone comes in. I don't want you meeting anyone in the waiting room."

When Detective Kelly was gone, Taperelli started thinking. He had nothing to do with Herbie's disappearance. He could say that with complete assurance. But he couldn't be so sure that it had nothing to do with Detective Kelly. He was handling this case for Jules Kenworth because he was Jules Kenworth's right-hand man. But if Ken-

225

worth didn't think he was doing the job adequately, Kenworth wasn't above getting someone else.

Taperelli called Mookie. "Did you find the girl?"

"Her name is Melanie Porter. According to her doorman, she works at Cornell Hospital. We followed her there earlier. Chico's sitting on her now."

"He won't lose her?"

"Not a chance. He's got a thing for girls in scrubs."

"She's a nurse?"

"An intern. Which is like a nurse, only different. It doesn't matter. They all wear scrubs."

"Just be careful you aren't seen. And don't lose her!"

"Don't worry. We'll grab her the minute she comes out the door."

Fred Flicker, Stone's factotum, was an unprepossessing man who doubled as a driver and bodyguard, though he seldom had to resort to weapons. A former member of the Royal Marines, Fred could barrel through larger opponents as if they weren't even there. Driving Stone's custom-made, armor-plated Bentley, he was invulnerable.

Stone might as well have been riding in a tank.

Stone called Fred into his office. "I need you to pick up an intern at Cornell Hospital."

"Oh?"

"A young lady by the name of Melanie Porter. She's a friend of our house guest. Given the manner in which Herbie's fiancée met her untimely end, I'd like you to be on your guard. Herbie likes this woman. I don't want to overlook the obvious."

Stone didn't add that this particular girl was also the sister of the man Herbie was defending, but it was certainly on his mind.

55

Dino put a rush on the Yvette Walker investigation so all reports came straight to him. It didn't take long to get results. The crime scene unit had lifted prints from the empty cash box in Herbie's walk-in closet. They ran the prints and got a match: Donald Dressler, aka Donnie Dressler, aka Iggy Dressler, aka Simon Covington, aka Lonnie LeBlanc, a small-time con man with multiple arrests and convictions, who only managed to stay out of jail by ratting on his friends.

Dino didn't bother to go through channels. He checked the lead out himself. The doorman at Herbie's building had no trouble picking Donnie out from the row of photos Dino lined up on his desk.

"I recognize him. Food delivery guy. Took up a pizza."

"What time was this?"

The doorman grimaced. "That's tough.

We get deliveries all night. Early as five, late as midnight."

"Can you do a little better than that?"

"Not much. I really don't remember."

"Is there a security camera in the lobby?"

"Yes, there is."

The security camera footage showed the delivery boy with the pizza approaching the desk at 8:05. Donnie's features were discernible in the picture.

Dino went down to the courthouse and hunted up ADA Monahan. She was surprised to see him.

"Wow. A personal visit from the commissioner. Am I in trouble or something?"

"Why would you think that?"

"To rate such special attention. Or could it be that I'm prosecuting a friend of yours?"

"Well, you certainly charged one. I doubt if you'll wind up prosecuting him."

"Is that a veiled threat?"

"This is a courtesy call to let you know what the department is doing. We wouldn't want you to be uninformed."

"Heaven forbid."

"With regard to that very case you mentioned, there have been some rapid developments. A suspect has emerged by the name of Donald Dressler." Dino slid a copy of Donnie's rap sheet in front of her on the desk. "The crime scene unit found his fingerprints all over the cash box that had been looted in the apartment. Of course, there's no way to tell when those prints were made. However, the doorman has identified Mr. Dressler as the young man who was sent up to Herbie Fisher's apartment in the guise of a pizza deliveryman at eight-oh-five last night."

"You have got to be kidding."

"It's on the surveillance video. His face is plainly visible. Anyway, we'll be issuing an APB on him as a suspect in the Yvette Walker homicide, and since you already have a suspect charged with the crime, I wouldn't want to cause you any embarrassment."

Dierdre Monahan's face got hard. "Are you telling me to drop the charges against Herbie Fisher?"

"Absolutely not. It's entirely your business. I'm just telling you mine. Sometimes our business conflicts, but we're all on the same side."

Dierdre referred to the rap sheet. "This guy's a two-bit grifter. He doesn't kill people. He's a con man."

"He's been busted a number of times and he doesn't like it. Each time's a harder fall. Maybe he didn't want to stick around and get caught."

"Oh," Dierdre said sarcastically. "He's sick of short prison terms so he decided he'd risk life?"

"We're just starting to get the facts. They don't all add up yet."

"That's an understatement."

"Anyway, I wanted to give you the heads-up."

After Dino left, ADA Monahan sat staring at the rap sheet. She'd have to tell the DA about this new development. He wouldn't want her prosecuting a case she couldn't win, particularly one that might lay the office open to ridicule. A dismissal wouldn't be a bar to future prosecution. If she let Herbie go, she could always charge him again.

ADA Monahan scowled and reached for the phone.

56

Dino stopped off at Stone's to give him the news.

Stone was as incredulous as Monahan. "A thief did it?"

"That's what the evidence shows."

"That doesn't make any sense."

"It makes more sense than Herbie did it."

"Then it wasn't Taperelli."

"It doesn't look like it, which is a big weight off my mind. I've been kicking myself around all day."

"So has Herbie. He blames himself for Yvette's death."

"You want to tell him?"

"He's not going to believe you. He's going to think you're making it up."

"You can't make up fingerprints."

"Actually, you can. Lift 'em from one place and label 'em as coming from another."

"My detectives wouldn't do that."

"Oh? Including Detective Kelly?"

"Fuck you, too, Stone."

"Let's go tell him."

Herbie wasn't convinced. "Yvette was killed by a burglar?"

"It's possible," Dino said. "In any event, it appears you were robbed."

"Appears?"

"Do you have a cash box in your walk-in closet?"

"Yes."

"Anything in it?"

"I keep some cash on hand."

"How much?"

"A few thousand in hundred-dollar bills, just for emergencies."

"Any jewels in the jewelry case?"

"Cuff links. Tie clips. A couple of watches."

"There's every indication they were stolen at the same time Yvette was killed."

"She surprised a burglar? I don't understand."

"Nothing adds up because the stage was set. She was killed elsewhere, and put in the bed. The gun was put in your hand."

"Can you prove that?"

"I'm doing my damnedest. The point is no one thinks you did it anymore."

"But they did," Herbie said flatly.

Seeing that Dino's assurances weren't lifting Herbie's mood, Stone said, "Most importantly, it looks like this had nothing to do with the court case. Taperelli, the detective, that's not what this was about. It just happened."

"Yes, but why?"

Dino shook his head. "I don't know. But I mean to find out."

57

Chico and Gus were parked outside the entrance of Cornell Hospital. Chico had found out when Melanie ended her shift, and brought in reinforcements. They'd come in a car in case she took a taxi home. Chico would follow her if she left on foot.

When the attractive blonde emerged from the hospital, Chico jabbed Gus in the ribs and pointed. "There she is."

Melanie was still in scrubs, but with a light jacket and carrying a purse. Instead of walking toward York Avenue, she headed for the circular driveway out front.

"She's going for the taxi line. You're up."

Gus started the engine.

There was one man ahead of Melanie waiting for a cab, and a woman was paying off a taxi by the curb. After he got that one, she'd be next.

Gus was revving the engine.

"You wanna tone it down? It's not a drag race."

Gus eased off the gas.

While they were watching, a sleek sedan squeezed past the taxi and slid to a stop in front of the hospital. The driver hopped out, came around, and ushered Melanie into the backseat.

"What the hell?" Chico murmured.

"Who is that?" Gus said.

"I don't know, but follow that car."

The Bentley took a surprisingly short trip, ending at a town house in Turtle Bay. Gus found it odd.

"Why pick her up in a private car to bring her a distance she could have walked?"

They watched as the Bentley pulled into an underground garage.

Chico pulled out his cell phone and called Mookie. "We couldn't get her."

"Why not?"

"A driver in a Bentley picked her up at the door and took her to a house in Turtle Bay."

"What's the address?"

Chico gave it. Mookie hung up the phone and cursed his luck. When things went bad, they went really bad. He had to hold it together. He couldn't afford to lose it, not on a job for a guy like Tommy Taperelli.

Mookie went to the computer and traced the ownership of the property. The town house was owned by a Mr. Stone Barrington. Wasn't that the lawyer who'd just showed up in court?

Mookie Googled him. Stone Barrington was indeed a lawyer. And not just any lawyer. Stone appeared to be one of the wealthiest, most well-connected men in America. He was reputed to cruise around in custom-made cars of his own specifications. If that was his car and driver, the girl would be impossible to abduct while she was under his protection. They'd have to wait until she went home and roust her out of her apartment.

Mookie bit the bullet and called Taperelli.

58

Melanie hugged Herbie in her arms. "You poor thing."

"I didn't do it."

"As if you had to tell me that. What a horrible thing. I'm so sorry about your fiancée."

"Why? You don't know me."

"True. I didn't even know you *had* a fiancée."

"It didn't come up."

"You must have loved her very much. I'm really sorry."

"Yeah."

"Do you want to talk about it? Do you want me to leave you alone? I just want to help, and I don't know how."

"Nothing helps."

"Of course not."

"I'm so confused. I came home. We were having drinks. The next thing I know I wake up in jail and am told I'm being charged with her murder."

"You blacked out?"

"I must have, but I don't know how. I only had one drink."

"Could you have been drugged?"

"That's what it was like. But it couldn't be."

"Are you sure?"

"The only one who could have drugged me was her."

Melanie thought that over. "Does this have anything to do with the case?"

"Why do you say that?"

"Your friend Stone sent his car just ten blocks to pick me up. I could easily have walked here. It got me wondering."

"He's overprotective. He means well. Why are you here?"

"I thought you might need a friend."

"I do," Herbie said. A tear welled in his eye.

Melanie held him again while he got control of himself. Then he pulled away and sat back.

"Now they think it was all a big mistake, that Yvette was killed by someone robbing the apartment."

"A robbery?"

"He took some jewelry and five thousand in cash. But why would he have to shoot her? Yvette wouldn't have tried to stop him."

"Maybe she could identify him."

"The *doorman* identified him. He walked right in. Didn't try to hide." Herbie heaved a sigh. "Anyway, if you're worried about your brother, I'll be back in court."

"I'm not worried about my brother. I mean, I am worried about my brother, but that's not why I'm here. Surely you know that."

"Well, he's still your brother. Don't worry, I will be in court tomorrow. And not just because of the bench warrant. I'll be in court because that's what lawyers do."

Melanie smiled and nodded, but she was hesitant.

Herbie picked up on it. "You think I'll be distracted. You think I won't be able to concentrate."

"No, I —"

Herbie put up his hand. "You're right. It'll be hard. I'm going to take Stone Barrington with me as second chair. He'll keep me focused."

"He doesn't know the case."

"He sent for the transcript. Tomorrow he'll know more about it than I do."

"I'm not worried about the case. I'm worried about you."

"I'll be fine," Herbie said.

But he didn't mean it.

59

Melanie came downstairs from Herbie's room.

"How's he doing?" Stone asked.

"Better. I'm going to go."

"Do you want a ride home?"

"Is that necessary?"

"No, I'm just offering."

"Why did you have me picked up at the hospital?"

Stone started to give her a vague answer, but changed his mind. This wasn't the type of girl to bullshit. "To keep you safe."

"Really?"

"Yes."

She smiled. "Now that I've seen Herbie, you don't care?"

"No, I don't think we need to anymore. When I sent the car, I thought this had to do with your brother's case. Apparently I was wrong. It now appears Yvette was killed during a robbery. There's a new suspect.

I'm perfectly happy to offer you a ride, but if you want to get home on your own power, I won't stop you."

"Thanks. I'd like to walk."

"Of course. Does he need anything?"

"I don't think so. Under the circumstances, he's doing well. Will he be here tomorrow?"

"He'll be in court tomorrow. After that, I imagine he'll be going home."

"Herb says you'll be in court, too."

"That's right. I'm already attorney of record. I was there this afternoon."

"Did you send for the transcripts?"

"How did you know?"

"He said you did."

"Herbie knows me well."

"Herbie?"

"That's what we used to call him. Before he got serious."

"Did you read the transcript?"

"Yes."

"And?"

"He made his point. The evidence indicates a police frame-up."

"Will the jury believe that?"

Stone shrugged. "That's another matter. Don't worry. We won't let you down."

Melanie nodded. "Okay. Thanks again."

60

Chico and Gus were succumbing to boredom outside Stone Barrington's town house. Neither was used to stakeouts, and they lacked the patience required. Gus was nearly asleep, while Chico fidgeted in his seat. When the front door finally opened and Melanie emerged, Chico jabbed Gus sharply in the ribs. "There she is."

Gus bolted upright "Alone?"

"Yeah."

"Good. Let's get her."

"Hang on. Don't start the engine, don't open the door. Let her walk away from the house. The place is a fucking fortress. We can't give her the chance to run back in."

Melanie walked down the street.

"Now?" Gus said.

"Hang on. See if anyone else comes out of the house."

No one did.

"All right, start it up. Follow me slowly."

Chico got out of the car and tailed Melanie down the street. He tried to catch up, but she was walking briskly and he didn't want to attract attention. Out of the corner of his eye he could see Gus pushing ahead of him in the car. That was all he needed, for the guy to spook her. He picked up the pace.

It wouldn't do to let her reach the corner. She wouldn't get away, he wasn't worried about that, but there was a greater chance they'd be seen. With a hop and a skip, he grabbed her by the arm.

Melanie whirled at his touch. She'd sensed his presence and was ready to act. Years of jujitsu didn't hurt. Medical school had cut short her martial arts training before she got her black belt, but she had her brown, and she was agile and quick.

She'd been prepared for some amorous drunk making a clumsy pass at her, so the sight of a large thug took her aback. So did his grip on her arm, which was rougher than that of your usual garden-variety creep.

She pretended to slip and drop to the ground. When he shifted his grip, she rolled sideways, sprang to her feet, and ran.

Gus, who'd followed them down the block, floored the accelerator and roared by. He threw the car into park and hopped out, blocking her escape.

Melanie, caught in the middle, darted up the alley between two brownstones. A wire fence blocked the end. Melanie leaped onto a garbage can and grabbed the top of the fence.

Chico caught her leg. He twisted and pulled down with all his weight. Gus grabbed her other leg. Chico shifted his grip to her arm and pried her fingers off the top of the fence.

Melanie bit his hand.

Chico howled in pain. He wrenched her free of the fence, slapped her across the face, and grabbed her in a bear hug even she couldn't break.

61

Chico called Mookie from the car. "We got her."

"Are you sure?"

"What do you mean, am I sure? She's in the fucking car."

"Are you sure it's her?"

"It's her. You showed me her picture."

Mookie had found the girl on Facebook and printed out her photo. He was more adept at a computer than he looked.

"All right. Come by and pick me up."

"We'll be there in five minutes."

Mookie was waiting at the corner when Gus pulled up.

"How did it go? Did anyone see you?"

"She's a wildcat," Chico said. "She bit my finger. But we weren't seen."

Gus went through the Midtown Tunnel and took the Long Island Expressway to Forest Hills, Queens, where he pulled up in front of a two-story frame house on a residential block.

"This is your cousin's place?"

"Yeah," Chico said.

"Take her in."

When Chico opened the trunk, Melanie kicked her tied-up legs and began yelling from behind the gag they'd put over her mouth. Hearing the commotion, Mookie came behind the car and looked down at her.

"I don't *need* you alive, sweetheart. Don't make your life more inconvenient than it's worth."

Cowed, Melanie fell limp as Chico and Gus lifted her out of the trunk and carried her up the front steps and in the front door. A couple of guys were hanging out in the living room. Mookie knew one of them. The other Chico introduced as his cousin Lou.

"There's your babysitters. There's a room upstairs that locks."

"Does it have a window?"

"It's nailed shut with railroad spikes."

"It's made of glass."

"She'd have to break a lot of small panes. The boys would hear her."

"Let's see it."

They pushed Melanie ahead of them up the stairs, toward a room at the end of the hall.

"In there," Lou said.

Mookie took a look around the room. It would do.

"Where's the bathroom?"

"Down the hall."

"How's she going to get there?"

"I'll take her."

"Let me see it."

Lou took them down the hall to the bathroom. The window was small. It would be tough to crawl out of open. Closed, with broken glass in the frame, it would be close to impossible.

The bathroom door had a lock that twisted shut from the inside. From the outside it opened with a key, but there was no key.

Mookie pointed to the door. "Take off the lock."

"Huh?"

"The lock on the door. Take it off."

"Why?"

"She smashes the window and calls for help, and you can't stop her because she locked the door. Just take it off."

"Okay," Lou said.

His attitude said he thought it was stupid.

62

Herbie woke up to a knock on his door. He rolled over and saw Helene coming in with a breakfast tray.

"Not hungry," he said.

She nodded. "That's what Stone said you'd say." She put the tray down on a side table. "He said to leave it anyway. You have to be in court at ten o'clock."

"What time is it?"

"Seven."

"Seven," Herbie muttered.

"He said you might not want to wear a sweat suit."

In a rush it all came back to him.

Herbie groaned. He sat up and groped for the coffeepot. He poured a cup, took a huge sip, and burned his tongue. He staggered into the bathroom and gulped some cold water.

Herbie stood under the shower for a long time. He had trouble finding the motivation to get out.

Eventually, he stumbled back into the bedroom and discovered he had no socks or underwear, or, if he did, he couldn't find them.

Herbie went downstairs and found Stone sitting at his desk.

"You *are* reading the transcript."

"Well, I'm trying. It's pretty boring, actually. Not your fault. Court transcripts *are* boring. But it's clear from this your client was framed."

"It is?"

"It is to me. You can't count on the jurors to follow the logic. Are you going home to change?"

"Yes, but I don't have any money."

"Check the pocket of your sweatpants. You should have enough to get you through the day."

Herbie put his hand in his pocket and pulled out a wad of cash. "Thanks, Stone."

Herbie went out and got a cab back to his apartment. It was strange walking into the building. The doorman didn't know what to say to him, and opted for saying nothing. That would have been fine with Herbie. Unfortunately, he needed a passkey. The doorman had to get it from the super, who wasn't in his apartment, so Herbie had to stand in the lobby in his sweats while the other tenants walked by.

Finally, he got the key, went upstairs, and opened the door.

He was almost afraid to go in.

He steeled himself, walked in, and went straight to the bedroom.

The bed had been stripped, but all traces of the crime scene unit were gone, with the exception of the small hole in the headboard where they'd dug out the bullet.

Herbie went into the living room to catch his breath.

His cell phone was lying on the coffee table. He picked it up and clicked it on. The battery was almost dead, but he had a message from around midnight. He called voice mail and listened through the interminable mechanical voice droning the date and the time.

Beep.

"We have your girlfriend. Lose the case, and lose it today."

Herbie dropped the phone as if it were hot.

63

Jules Kenworth was angry, even for him. "What the fuck do you guys think you're doing?" he yelled through the phone.

Taperelli was taken aback. "What's the matter?"

"What do you think is the matter? Jesus Christ, I ask you to do one simple thing."

"What simple thing?"

"Pick up the girl. That's all I said. Grab the girl."

"We did."

"Yeah. You did a slam-bang job."

Taperelli was becoming confused. "What do you mean?"

"She's dead! The headline's in this morning's *New York Post*! The girl is no good to me dead. You really fucked up this time." Taperelli heard a bang as Kenworth slammed the phone down.

Taperelli buzzed his secretary. "Drop what you're doing and run out and get a copy of the *New York Post.*"

Five minutes later she returned with the paper. The headline, LAWYER'S GIRL-FRIEND MURDERED, jumped off the front page.

Taperelli snatched up the phone and called Mookie. "Did you kill the girl?"

"What?"

"The lawyer's girlfriend. I told you to pick her up, not kill her."

"I didn't kill her."

"Then why's she dead?"

"She's not dead. Chico's holding her out in Queens."

"Oh, is that right?"

"Yeah. I took her there myself."

"When?"

"Last night."

"Alive?"

"Alive and kicking."

"You see the *New York Post*?"

"No, why?"

"The paper says she's dead."

"Bullshit. She's in Queens."

"Yeah, well, then someone's wrong. She can't be dead *and* in Queens."

"Why not? They got a cemetery."

"Get out there. Make sure she's alive."

"She's alive, all right."

"You sure she's the right girl?"

"Absolutely. I saw her myself. It's her, all right."

"Yeah, well, get out there and check on her. This fucking case is jinxed."

64

The medical examiner called Commissioner Dino Bacchetti with the autopsy report. "You wanted a heads-up on Yvette Walker. It's pretty straightforward. The girl was killed by a gunshot wound to the head. No contributing factors."

"She wasn't drugged?"

"No. Trace amounts of alcohol and that's it. On the other hand, the toxicology report on the man she was found with is off the chart."

"What?"

"You were right on the money with the knockout drops. Someone slipped your guy chloral hydrate, and a whacking dose of it. He's lucky he's not dead."

"Could you tell when it was administered?"

"Not long before the sample was taken. He still had a lot in his system."

"But the decedent didn't have any in her

bloodstream?"

"Like I said, trace amounts of alcohol and that's it."

"What about the time of death?"

"She was killed sometime between seven and nine o'clock."

"Based on what?"

"Body temperature, largely."

"What about the stomach contents?"

"Doesn't narrow it down. She was killed five or six hours after eating what appears to be a Cobb salad."

"What about pizza?"

"What about it?"

"Was there any in the stomach contents?"

"Nope. Just salad."

"There's no chance she had a slice of pizza shortly before she died?"

"No, there isn't. I can't speak for the gentleman involved. He only had a blood test."

Dino had barely hung up the phone when it rang again.

It was Herbie.

"Dino. Thank God. I went back to my apartment to get clothes for court."

"You're still going to court?"

"Yeah, yeah. Listen. I had a voice mail on my cell phone, came in about midnight last night. It said I better lose the court case because they had my girlfriend."

Dino blinked. "Is that right?"

"There was no number, just the message and that's it."

"Midnight last night?"

"According to the voice mail."

"That makes no sense at all."

"No kidding."

"Go to court. Act as if nothing happened. Let me handle it."

"How can you handle it? What is there to handle?"

"Let me worry about that. You just get ready for court."

Dino hung up and called Stone. "I think Herbie's losing it."

"Can you blame him?"

"No, he just called me and said he got an anonymous phone call saying his girlfriend's been kidnapped."

"What?"

"I know, it makes no sense. He said they threatened to kill her if he doesn't lose the case. Do you think there's a chance Yvette's death had to do with the case after all?"

"How would the con man fit in? And why would they make the threat after she's already dead?"

"I have no idea."

"Well, I wish I could be more help, but I

have to be in court."

"You seen the *New York Post*?"

"Why?"

"It's on the front page. Lawyer's girlfriend murdered. You can bet at least half of the jurors will have seen it."

"Does it mention Herbie?"

"Says he was questioned as a suspect. The fact that the police are now looking for another suspect didn't make the cut."

"Has Herbie seen it?"

"He didn't say. But he had other things on his mind."

Stone sighed. "Oh, Christ. He's probably the only one in New York who hasn't."

65

Stone Barrington arrived at court to find Herbie there already.

"Are you all right?" Stone said.

"No, but I managed to tie my tie. This morning I'm a nervous wreck."

"I can take the cross."

"What does it matter? If I don't dump the case, they'll kill my dead girlfriend."

"Dino told me. He's on it. We need to concentrate on winning this case."

"Are you saying I can't?"

"I'm sure you can if you're not inhibited by an empty threat."

The jurors were led in. It was clear from their posture that most of them had either read or heard of the story in the *Post*. Before the witness was returned to the stand, Stone Barrington stood up to address the court.

"Your Honor, I have a motion that should be made in chambers."

Judge Buckingham glared down at the defense table. "We have already wasted a full day of the court's time. I think we should proceed."

Stone Barrington's eyes twinkled. "Would you like me to make this motion in open court, Your Honor?"

Judge Buckingham could not think of a proper rebuke. "Attorneys. In my chambers," he snapped, and slammed the gavel down.

When they were all assembled in chambers, Judge Buckingham said, "What is it now?"

"Your Honor," Stone said, "the *New York Post* has a front-page story saying that Mr. Fisher's girlfriend has been murdered, and that he is being questioned as a suspect in the crime. Under the circumstances, you can hardly expect the jurors to render a fair and impartial verdict in this case. I ask you to declare a mistrial, dismiss the jury, and postpone proceedings until we can impanel an impartial jury."

"I had a feeling that was the motion you were about to make. The jurors have been instructed not to read or listen to any news stories relating to the crime. There is no reason to suppose that they have disobeyed the court's order. The motion is denied."

"The jurors wouldn't know this article had any bearing on the case until they read it, Your Honor. At which point the harm would be done."

"The only way to tell would be to question the jurors. If they didn't know before, they'd know then. I'm not going to deliberately create a mistrial. I have already denied your motion. If you persist in pursuing this, you will be in contempt of court."

Judge Buckingham turned on his heel and strode from chambers.

"What do we do now?" Herbie said.

"Relax," Stone said. "I'll take the cross."

When the lawyers were back in court and Detective Kelly had been returned to the stand, Judge Buckingham said, "Does the defense have any further questions for this witness?"

Stone stood up. "The defense does, Your Honor."

In the back of the courtroom, a tough-looking thug got up and walked out.

66

A cab pulled up to Cousin Lou's house in Queens. Mookie got out, told the driver to wait, and went in.

Lou was asleep on the couch. Mookie gave it a kick. Cousin Lou woke with a start and sat up, rubbing his eyes.

"What the fuck?"

"Where's the girl?"

"Upstairs."

"How do you know?"

"She's locked in."

"When did you see her last?"

"This morning. I took her to the bathroom."

"Let's go."

Cousin Lou led the way upstairs and unlocked the door.

Melanie was sitting on the bed. She sprang up when the door opened, but shied back when she saw it was Mookie. He walked in, took ahold of her chin, and twisted her face up to look at him.

"Who are you?"

She pulled away and glared at him.

"Come on, honey. What's your name?"

"Melanie Porter."

"You're Herb Fisher's girlfriend."

"No."

"No?"

"No."

"But you know him."

"He's my brother's attorney."

Mookie's eyes widened. "Really? Who's your brother?"

"David Ross."

A grin spread over Mookie's face. "Is that so?" He jerked his thumb at Lou. "Lock her up. Call your cousin. I want at least two guys here at all times. Preferably three. And stay awake."

As soon as he was out the front door, Mookie whipped out his cell phone and called Taperelli.

"I think we just hit the jackpot."

Jules Kenworth digested the information. "Run that by me again."

Taperelli spoke with glee. "We got the councilman's daughter. We thought she was the lawyer's girlfriend because he'd taken her out. We didn't peg her as the councilman's daughter because she's got a different name — Melanie Porter. You wouldn't know her father was Ross."

"She's the councilman's little girl?"

"Yeah. Isn't that great? As long as we're holding her, the old man's going to do what we want. Now you don't even need a verdict. We just hang on to her until after the vote."

"That works this time, for this vote, but I need Ross to approve everything I do. I want his kid in jail so he *always* votes my way."

"I understand."

"Then do it."

67

Melanie couldn't get out. She'd come to that conclusion not without considerable experimentation. The window in the room was indeed nailed shut. There was no way she was moving the railroad spikes, even if she had something to pry them with, which she didn't. If by some miracle she did manage to get the window open, she would face a two-story drop onto solid concrete. There was only a bare wall, nothing to climb down. As for smashing a pane and calling out, the window faced the back alley, not the street. There was no corresponding window in the house beyond, and the chances of anyone hearing her were nil.

The window was the only possible means of escape except for the door, which was always locked, except when that moron took her to the bathroom. Lou, as she'd heard them call him, wasn't very big, but he had a gun. He always had it out when he opened the door, not like he needed it, but like he got a thrill out of carrying it. His lack of expertise was not comforting. He looked like he could shoot her by mistake.

Melanie was pretty sure she could overpower Lou if it weren't for the gun. Just the element of surprise would give her the advantage, but she had to be a little more desperate before she tried it. And the longer she waited, the less he'd be expecting it.

The door opened and Melanie looked up from the bed. A thug stuck his head in the door and said, "Bathroom."

It wasn't Lou. It was another guy, slightly bigger, probably of equal intelligence. And he didn't have a gun.

Melanie's pulse quickened. If she was ever going to make a move, the time was now.

She got up from the bed, dispiritedly, and trudged out the door.

He walked behind her to the bathroom. She measured his steps. She spun suddenly, grabbed his wrist, and pulled down. Her other hand chopped down on his forearm.

He pulled back in pain and surprise.

She kicked him full out in the balls.

He doubled up in pain, and she dashed by him and darted down the stairs.

Lou was lounging on the couch. He lunged to his feet, grabbing for his gun.

She ran by him. The front door was unlocked. She flung it open, dashed out into the street, and yelled, "Help!" at the top of her lungs.

No one heard, no windows opened, no one came out any door, except for the armed thug who was right on her heels.

She reached the corner and turned right.

A car was coming down the street. There were two men in the front seat. Lou wouldn't shoot her in front of witnesses. She ran straight at the car, waving her arms frantically.

The driver hit the brakes and skidded to a stop.

Chico and Gus got out of the car. Chico had a gun in his hand. He pointed it at her, looked at Lou, who was doubled up out of breath, and shook his head in disgust.

He swung the butt of the gun at her head and knocked her out.

68

Councilman Ross got the call on his lunch break. He'd have gotten it sooner, but he couldn't take calls in court. He was just coming down the steps when his phone rang.

It was his secretary. She'd been calling him every five minutes.

"You're about to get a phone call. Make sure you answer."

"Of course."

"It's important."

"I'll take it."

"Please. I've got a bad feeling."

"What are you talking about?"

"A man called, insistent, asking to speak to you immediately. When I said you were in court, he didn't seem to understand that your phone wasn't on, got quite angry."

"Maybe it was just a crank."

"I don't think so. This was scary. Answer your phone."

The line beeped.

"This must be it." Ross switched the call. "Yes?"

It was a male voice, hostile and threatening. "Councilman. I understand you've been in court. This is not good. The case should be over."

"Who is this?"

"A fan. I like your work. I'd like to see it continue."

"I'm hanging up now."

"That would be a mistake. Do you care about your children?"

"What about my children?"

"Well, your son's on trial, and your daughter isn't. Who do you think is in the most danger?"

"Now, look here —"

"No, *you* look here. I'm telling you how it is, and how it's gonna be. If you care for your children, you're going to listen hard and you're not going to get it wrong. Here's the situation. It's very simple, but it's very important, so pay attention. This is a matter for you and not for the police. Should the police become involved, the story would be over, and it will not have a happy ending. The story will only have a happy ending if we keep this to ourselves. This is just between you and me."

There was a pause, and then the ultima-tum.

"Your daughter's not coming home until your son's case is lost. If he wins the case, she's not coming home at all."

69

Councilman Ross called his daughter. It went to voice mail. He left a message. "Melanie, it's Dad. Call me back as soon as you get this."

He hung up and called his secretary. "I need to speak to Melanie. She's not answering her phone. Call the hospital, find out when she went to work and when she gets off. Leave a message for her. If you get her on the phone, I need to speak to her immediately."

"Yes, sir."

She called back in ten minutes. "She didn't come in today."

"At all?"

"No. No one's seen her since last night. She was supposed to be on shift today but never showed. I left messages in case she does come in, but she's not there."

Councilman Ross hung up and hurried down the street to the little diner where he and Herbie had had lunch. Herbie was in a booth with David and Stone Barrington. They asked him to join them, but he waved it away.

"I have to talk to Herb."

Herbie got up from his seat. The councilman practically pulled him outside.

"What's up?" Herbie said.

"Melanie's missing."

"What?"

"I just got a phone call saying she won't be home until we lose the case. And if we win the case, she won't be home at all."

"You mean Taperelli has got her?"

"That's what it looks like. She's not answering her phone, and she didn't show up for work."

"We've got to go to the police."

"They'll kill her if we do."

"Stone Barrington's friends with the police commissioner. They can be discreet."

"The police framed my son. Do you think they wouldn't know?"

"What do you want to do?"

"They said to lose the case."

"Do you want your son in jail?"

"Of course I don't want my son in jail."

"Okay, so we don't finish the case. They're not going to hurt her until the case is over."

"Yes, but it has to be soon. If we stall,

they'll hurt her."

Herbie exhaled noisily and thought that over. "Okay. That's the situation. We can't finish the case, and we can't stall."

"That's what I've been telling you," Councilman Ross said. "How are you going to handle that?"

Herbie smiled grimly. "Just watch me."

70

When court reconvened Herbie said, "Let me take the witness."

"Are you sure?" Stone said.

"Let me take a shot. You can always stop me if I go far afield."

Stone hesitated. Having read the transcript, Stone considered Herbie's whole cross-examination far afield. "Fine. If you flounder, I'm jumping in."

Judge Buckingham banged the gavel. "Gentlemen. Do you have any more questions for this witness?"

Herbie stood up and approached the stand. "I'm almost done with this witness, Your Honor. Just one or two more questions."

"Proceed."

"Detective, we're almost done. I have just one small matter to clear up while you're on the stand. How did you know that the defendant would be selling drugs at the party?"

The detective hesitated. "From intelligence received from the narcotics division."

"The narcotics division is tough to subpoena, Detective. What *person* informed you the defendant would be there?"

"I would have to consult my notes."

"Your Honor, I ask that the detective be given time to consult his notes before I continue my cross-examination."

"Detective Kelly, how long will it take you to consult your notes?"

"Some little while, Your Honor. My notes are back at the precinct."

"There is no one else with that information in court?"

"Your Honor," Herbie said, "are you suggesting I rely on secondhand hearsay information from a person not even under oath?"

"I am not, Mr. Fisher, and you know it. Detective, you are excused to get your notes. Please get all your notes. Everything you could possibly need to complete your testimony. Bring it to the courthouse tomorrow morning at ten o'clock.

"We are about to adjourn. Jurors are admonished once again not to talk about

the case. Court is adjourned until tomorrow morning at ten o'clock."

71

Tommy Taperelli was supervising a shipment down by the docks. There was no danger in doing so because there was no contraband on board. Somewhere between Colombia and the Jersey Shore, several kilos of cocaine had been removed and replaced with baby laxative. This was not unheard of. Tommy Taperelli's coke was always cut with baby laxative, only it was cut *after* it arrived, increasing his profits as much as twofold. The shipment in question had been cut *before* it arrived, decreasing the value of the product he had bought.

The substitution might have gone unnoticed had not Tommy Taperelli had a chemist standing by in the warehouse to test the coke as soon as it arrived. After testing samples from several kilos, the chemist was able to report back to Tommy Taperelli that the product in question had a ninety-nine percent chance of proving effective in the case of a constipated baby.

Hence Tommy's visit to the ship.

Taperelli was having a chat with the captain, a swarthy man with scraggly black hair and a beard, who was proclaiming his innocence. "I'm the captain. I run the ship. I don't handle the cargo."

"Who does?"

"Emilio."

Emilio, a skinny young Colombian with greasy hair and shifty eyes, also disavowed all knowledge, but had no one to pass the buck to.

Taperelli let Emilio protest until it became boring, then told two of his henchmen to "show him the bill of lading," and they walked him away.

Show him the bill of lading was a euphemism. Emilio wasn't coming back.

Taperelli was coming down the gangplank when his phone rang.

It was Mookie, calling from court. "Bad news."

Taperelli couldn't believe it. "*We're* stalling?"

"It's that fucking detective," Mookie said. "He asked for an adjournment."

"Why would he do that?"

"The lawyer finessed him. Asked him something he didn't know. Something he'd

278

have to look up. Here's the lawyer saying I want to wind up my testimony. Here's the detective saying I have to consult my notes."

"What notes? Why does he need notes?"

"The lawyer wants to know who told him the guy would be at the party."

"Oh, shit."

"That's a problem."

"Damn right it's a problem. No one told him the guy would be there. He picked him up and he followed him there."

"Why doesn't he just say that?"

"He already said he was there because the guy was selling drugs at the party. The question is who told him that?"

"What's the answer?"

"How the fuck should I know?"

"Okay, what do you want me to do?"

"I don't know. Has the lawyer left yet?"

"No. I came right out."

"He's the guy who asked the question, right? Not the other guy?"

"No. Herb Fisher."

"Yeah. The pain in the ass. Keep tabs on him. The guy might have an accident."

"Really?"

"Better him than me. If I can't straighten this out, it's going to get ugly."

The phone bleeped. It was Detective Kelly. "We got troubles."

"I heard."

"What do you want me to do?"

"Tell the truth."

"Huh?"

"The guy wants to know who told you the defendant would be at the party?"

"Yeah."

"Tell him no one did. You were acting on intel drugs were being sold there. You checked it out, and this is the guy who was selling 'em."

"I like it."

"I hate it. I want you off the stand. Don't let him screw you with a follow-up."

Taperelli walked out to the end of the pier. He looked out across the ocean and took a deep breath of the salt air.

Now for the call he didn't want to make.

72

Someone was going to get fired. That was all there was to it. A head was going to roll. Jules Kenworth was at the mayor's luncheon, but he wasn't at the mayor's table. That was completely unacceptable. It was embarrassing. It was demeaning. It was the type of thing that should not happen, could not happen. And there was nothing he could do about it. He could get up and walk out, but that would only underline the situation. Or he could sit there and pray that damn photographer from the *Daily News* wouldn't catch him in the background in a shot of the mayor's table.

Yes, heads were going to roll. Either his own secretary, or the mayor's damn booking agent, who put him there just to be mean. He could imagine her doing it, too, the vindictive bitch. Just because he'd once groped her in the elevator. The elevator was crowded, and his hand may have been on her leg, but where the hell was he supposed to put it?

His cell phone rang, a welcome interruption that would allow him to gracefully exit. He could take an important call, ignoring the lesser lights at his table. He could see the headline: JULES KENWORTH MOVES MILLIONS AT MAYOR'S LUNCHEON.

He took out the phone and looked at caller ID. Tommy Taperelli. Under normal circumstances, a call from a mob boss was something Jules Kenworth would flaunt. Today it had bad connotations.

He clicked on the phone. "Give me good news."

"They adjourned for the day."

Kenworth stood up so fast his chair tipped over. Everyone at his table looked at him. People at the mayor's table looked at him. The mayor looked at him.

Kenworth made the most of the moment. He covered the phone, smiled to the room in general, and announced, "I'm sorry. I just lost a hundred million dollars. No big deal. Just an annoyance. I'll take it outside."

Kenworth pushed out the swinging door into the hallway. "What the hell is going on? Did you talk to the councilman?"

"I did."

"And he defied you?"

"No, he didn't."

Taperelli told Kenworth what had transpired in court.

Kenworth wasn't impressed. "How the hell did you let this get away from you? I thought you had clout. You can't even keep your own men in line."

"The detective panicked. He wasn't expecting the question."

"Do I care? I'm not asking you for excuses. I'm asking you for results. If you can't deliver, I will get someone else. I thought you were the best."

"I *am* the best."

"Then I'd hate to see the worst."

Kenworth realized he'd gone too far. Taperelli was not just any mob boss. He was special. At least, he thought he was. He'd only take so much abuse before throwing in the towel and walking away.

"Look. I created a scene at my table. Then I apologized, saying I'd just lost a hundred million dollars, and laughed it off as if it were nothing. Well, it isn't nothing. And when I said it, I didn't know it was true. If this doesn't come off, a hundred million is going to look like chickenfeed. I am going to lose a hell of a lot more than that. So tell me, how are we going to fix this?"

"You've got the girl. The councilman's going to vote the way you want. Why the hurry to convict the kid?"

"If the kid isn't convicted, you gotta hold the girl until the vote. The longer you hold her, the bigger the risk. You hold on to the girl, *you're* vulnerable. You put the kid in jail, *he's* vulnerable. I want *him* vulnerable. Put him in jail, release the girl, no one can touch us."

Kenworth clicked the phone off and went back to lunch, thinking of what bullshit story he should tell them. The bottom line was his cunning and brilliance had averted a hundred-million-dollar loss and turned it into a profit. The details didn't matter. They wouldn't understand them anyway. Kenworth was grinning as he pushed his way through the door.

73

Herbie had to get away. He was being pulled in too many directions. Stone wanted to help him win the case. The councilman wanted him to lose the case. His client wanted to know what was going on. His client's sister had been kidnapped and he couldn't tell anyone. And his girlfriend had been killed, apparently by a sneak thief who had nothing to do with any of all that. And James Glick, the guy who got him into it all, had disappeared off the face of the earth, and probably wasn't coming back.

If he told Dino, even in confidence, Melanie Porter was as good as dead. At least that's what her father thought, and Herbie wasn't going to go against his wishes. Not the way his luck had been running. Ever since this case began it had been one disaster after another.

Herbie had to walk and clear his head, get away from the constant questions being thrown at him, so he'd have time to concentrate on his own. He headed for the East River. He'd walk uptown, along the bank, until something came to him. In all probability, he'd walk all the way home.

Herbie didn't even notice the limo cruising along beside him, not until the doors flew open and Carlo descended on him. It was more than he could take. If he'd had a gun, he'd have pulled it. He was lucky he didn't.

He was flung into the limo. Mario Payday sat in the backseat, puffing on a big cigar. It was stifling in the car with the windows up and the cloud of smoke, but no one was complaining.

Mario shook his head disapprovingly. "Mr. Fisher. I hardly thought that I'd be seeing you again."

"What do you want?"

"So rude? That's uncalled for, Mr. Fisher. I understand you've had a hard time, but that does not relieve you of your obligation to me. You owe me ninety thousand dollars, Mr. Fisher, and the last time I checked, you had not paid."

"Oh, for Christ's sake."

"I'm sorry about your fiancée. A most unfortunate occurrence. Surely the police have come to their senses and realized that was not your fault. Any money you had tied up in bail would be returned. And it couldn't have come at a better time. When you have a pressing obligation."

"I can't deal with this now."

"Mr. Fisher, you have had several days. Much longer than any of my other clients. Indeed, were it to get around that I am allowing people several days, it would hurt my reputation. I am Mario Payday. I am not Mario Pay-me-in-a-few-days-when-it's-convenient."

"I don't have the money."

"You have plenty of money. You won the jackpot in the Lotto. Even you, my reckless friend, have not managed to run through all of it. You have more than enough money left to settle your debts."

"I can't touch it."

"What?"

"I can't touch the money. I have a conservator. Any expenses must be justified."

"I find that hard to believe, Mr. Fisher. Why in the world would you allow that?"

"I bought a penthouse apartment on Park Avenue and the condo board didn't like the rate at which my money was decreasing."

Mario shrugged. "Condo boards can be difficult."

"This one is. And I have a problem with

my conservator."

"Why not simply explain the philosophy of Mario Payday?"

"He's not familiar with it."

"That's a shame. It's something everyone should learn. You're a lawyer, are you not, Mr. Fisher?"

"I am."

Mario grimaced, held up his hand. "That's where your story doesn't ring true. A lawyer can sell anything. That's what he does. I can't believe you can't come up with a pressing need for ninety thousand dollars that your conservator would go for. Assuming *that* story is true, and not just the wild concoction of a desperate lawyer."

Herbie smiled. "Would I lie to you?"

74

Mookie, who had trailed Herbie from the courthouse, watched as his target was hauled into a limo by two large goons. He called Taperelli from across the street. "The lawyer's in a limo with Mario Payday."

"Are you sure?"

"I didn't see Mario, but Carlo and Ollie the Ox walked him in. They're Mario's boys, so it's gotta be him."

"The lawyer must owe him money."

"I don't know how. Guy's a lawyer, for Christ's sakes. Maybe it's something else."

"No," Taperelli said, "with Mario Payday it's always money. That's interesting. Mario must have killed his girlfriend."

"What?"

"Mario's not subtle. Mr. Fisher owes him cash. He didn't pay. Mario killed his girl and now he's squeezing him. That's the way he plays."

"It's gotta be a shitload of money."

"Yes, it does."

"What do you want me to do?"

"Make sure he gets *out* of the limo and back home intact. Mario's been known to cut his losses just to make a point."

"Hard to imagine if the debt's as big as you think. A guy could retire on just the interest."

"Just make sure."

"Hang on. It looks like he's getting out now."

The back door of the limo opened and Herbie stepped out, looking grim and determined.

Mookie wondered what he'd been told.

Herbie paid no attention to anyone, just trudged blindly down the street.

"He let him go," Mookie said. "The guy looks defeated. I think he's walking home."

"Make sure."

"If he goes home, can we leave it at that?"

"If he stays there."

75

Donnie was drinking the good stuff. He could afford it now. He'd never had so much money. And Yvette was dead, so he didn't have to split it. Not that he'd wanted her dead, but he couldn't deny the material benefits. He sat in the bar on Sixth Avenue drinking Johnnie Walker Black. He'd already had three, so the quality of the scotch didn't matter to him. He could have been drinking standard rotgut and it would have tasted the same. But why should he? It was worth it just for the kick he got out of telling the bartender, "Johnnie Walker Black."

Five thousand in cash. Too bad it was all in hundreds. He'd have to break a bill here, break a bill there. Never enough to raise suspicion, to call attention to himself.

The television over the bar was showing the news. Donnie couldn't care less about the news. He was waiting for the sports. He finally had enough money to place a few bets, and not the rinky-dink, ten-bucks-to-win, dollar-box bets he usually put on the ponies. He could play a ten-dollar box, put a hundred bucks on the nose. He could throw in a few basketball games to boot. Donnie could imagine that bookie's eyes bugging out of his head.

That sexy anchor Donnie liked was back with a news story. He wondered whose girlfriend she was to get that cushy job. Nice-looking, but not a great speaking voice. She clearly had other talents.

"The police have a new suspect in the murder of a Park Avenue socialite. What was originally thought to be a lovers' quarrel is now being deemed a robbery/murder, and a manhunt is on for the suspect."

A close-up of Donnie's mug shot filled the screen.

"The fugitive, Donald Dressler, is suspected of killing the decedent, Yvette Walker, when she surprised him in the act of robbing the apartment in which she resided with her fiancé, Herb Fisher, a prominent attorney with Woodman & Weld. According to the police, Mr. Dressler escaped with some priceless jewelry and approximately five thousand dollars in hundred-dollar bills. The police are warning viewers to be on the lookout for a young man of his description attempting to pass hundred-dollar bills."

Donnie snatched the hundred-dollar bill he'd been planning to use for his drinks off the counter and replaced it with three twenties. He chugged his scotch, keeping his head down, and walked unobtrusively out of the bar.

On the sidewalk his heart was thumping. How had they gotten on to him so fast?

He had to get out of there, and fast. If it were winter, he could pull a ski cap down over his forehead, but it was summer, and he didn't even have a baseball cap. A beard would be nice, but it would take a while to grow. He needed sunglasses. There was a Ray-Ban store up the street. He could buy a pair there, but he'd have to pay with a hundred-dollar bill.

He had to get out of town. That was just a local news report. No one outside New York City would have seen it. Anywhere else he'd be safe. He couldn't fly, they'd ask him for ID, but he could buy a train ticket with cash.

Donnie cut over to Seventh Avenue and headed for Penn Station.

76

Detective Brogan knocked on the door of the commissioner's office and walked in. Dino's secretary had already announced him.

Dino waved him over to the desk. "You got something, Detective?"

"Yes, sir. You wanted everything you could get on Donnie Dressler."

"You got something new?"

"I got something that isn't on the rap sheet."

"Oh?"

"His last two convictions he was suspected of working with an unnamed accomplice. The accomplice wasn't charged because he didn't give her up. He didn't *need* to give her up because he'd already rolled on somebody else. In one instance, Fred Walsh, in the other, Paul Peretti. In both cases the, quote, co-conspirator, unquote, claimed to barely know Donald Dressler, though each was alleged to be helping to fence stolen goods and caught with some of the contraband. Both said he was reputed to have worked with an attractive young lady who hooked the victims before Dressler ripped them off."

"I don't suppose you got a name?"

"They didn't have a name, and it probably wouldn't be hers."

"Description?"

"Young, baby-faced blonde."

"You speak to these guys?"

"No, just the ADAs in charge."

"Where are they now?"

"In jail. Which tells you something, huh? Principal walks and they're in jail. Twice, for Christ's sakes. For two separate crimes. You'd think they'd be pretty pissed."

"Talk to them, will you? Get more on Dressler, and more on the girl. Show them a picture of Yvette Walker while you're at it."

"You think it's her?"

"Be nice if something in this damn case added up."

77

Detective Brogan called Dino from the prison. "I spoke to both of them. They hate Dressler, naturally enough, and would love to see him go down. I had to listen to them saying they'd been framed, which they all say, but I kind of believe them. That Dressler is a nasty son of a bitch."

"What about the girl?"

"Well, that's the thing. Fred Walsh was sure Dressler worked with a female accomplice and identified a photo of Yvette Walker as being her."

"Really?"

"Yeah, but I don't think it means anything. The guy's saying whatever he thinks we want to hear. You know, hoping we'll put in a good word with the parole board."

"He didn't pick her out of a lineup?"

"No, that's my fault. He wasn't ID'ing a suspect, just the victim. It was only after he did it I began to doubt the identification."

"What about the other guy?"

"Paul Peretti is another story. He didn't know much, but he wasn't trying to sell me anything. He picked the girl out of a row of five pictures, but he didn't know that much about her. He'd seen him with her once, but that was it. He'd heard the guy worked with a female accomplice, but he didn't know if that was her. It's not that helpful, but for what it's worth, I consider his opinion solid."

"Thanks, Detective. For what it's worth, I consider *your* opinion solid."

Dino called Stone and told him what he'd just heard.

"So what do you think?" Stone said.

"As far as I'm concerned, it's conclusive. It's the only thing that makes sense. He's delivering a pizza. He calls upstairs, the girl says sure, bring it up. Well, no one ate any pizza, no one ordered any pizza, the damn thing was a prop. Just an empty box with a few crusts. That only makes sense if they were working together. It also explains the knockout drops. She drugged Herbie so her boyfriend could rip the place off."

"So what do you want to do?"

"We have to tell him."

"I'd like to have more proof."

"We're not going to get it."

"Probably not," Stone said. "When do you want to do it?"

"Let's take him out to dinner."

"Really?"

"He's all alone in that apartment. It can't be good for him."

"Okay. Thanks, Dino. I'll take care of it."

78

Herbie didn't want to go out to dinner, but he couldn't talk his way out of it. Under the circumstances, there was nothing he could say that didn't convince Stone he *needed* cheering up. Still, the only reason he gave in was Stone was so insistent Herbie had the feeling they had something to tell him.

It turned out to be true. Once they had settled with their drinks and ordered a round of steaks for all, Dino told him what he'd learned.

Herbie couldn't believe it. "She was working with the robber?"

"That's what it looks like."

"So why did he kill her?"

"We don't know."

"It makes no sense."

"It's the answer to who drugged your drink."

"Are you sure my drink was drugged?"

"I tested your blood."

"Did you test hers?"

"She wasn't drugged."

"I don't understand."

Herbie's cell phone rang. He jerked it out of his pocket and clicked it on. "Hello?"

"Mr. Fisher, we have a problem. What part of 'no cops' didn't you understand?"

Herbie was aware of Stone's and Dino's eyes on him, as he spoke to the man he knew must work for Tommy Taperelli. He said casually, "I understand."

"You're having dinner with the commissioner of police."

"I'm out with Stone and Dino. They're trying to take my mind off things."

"I assume you spoke to the councilman. Anything he told you is strictly confidential."

"At the moment, I can't even think about business."

"Think about this. What I told the councilman goes double for you. If you *mention* his daughter, you won't be *seeing* his daughter. Capiche?"

"I have to be in court tomorrow morning. I hope to be back in the office tomorrow afternoon."

"That's the ticket. Play it like that and no one gets hurt."

The line clicked dead.

Herbie put the phone back in his pocket.

"Who's that?" Dino said.

"Bill Eggers. Wants to know when I'll be back to work."

"Does he know your fiancée was just killed?" Stone said.

"*I* don't know my fiancée was just killed," Herbie said. "According to Dino, she was a con artist. Was her name even Yvette?"

"That part *was* true. Yvette Walker. It was on her rap sheet."

"She had a rap sheet?"

"Yes."

"For ripping guys off?"

"No. For prostitution."

Herbie sighed. "Oh, for Christ's sake. I'm like a three-time loser who can't break away. You try to go straight and get sucked back into the life."

"You get any more crank phone calls?" Dino said.

Dino was really just changing the subject, but after Taperelli's phone call, the question threw Herbie. He blinked. "Huh?"

"I don't think you will. That had to be Taperelli's men trying to scare you. They hadn't seen the news in the paper yet. Now that they have, they won't call again."

"That's more proof the burglar did it," Stone said. "The threatening phone call proves it wasn't them."

Herbie sighed deeply, rubbed his forehead.

"Sorry," Dino said. "I know you don't want to talk about it."

"I'm okay," Herbie said. "It's just so much to take in."

The food arrived and the waiter slid the plates onto the table.

"Eat your steak," Stone said.

"I'll try," Herbie said. He smiled gamely. "I doubt if I'll be able to taste it."

Stone grinned at him over his mouthwatering mountain of meat. "I beg to differ."

79

Mookie called Taperelli back. "You spoke to him?"

"Yeah."

"And?"

"I think he's clean. Just a case of friends taking him out to dinner. Did they react while he was on the phone?"

"Not at all," Mookie said. "He played it very cool. He might have been confirming a business appointment."

"I think it's okay. I think he's scared to death, particularly after what happened to his girlfriend. He's not going to put another girl at risk."

"So it's just another ordinary dinner?"

"Looks like it."

"So can I knock off?"

"If he goes home, sure. Just so he don't go anywhere else."

Mookie was pissed when he hung up the phone. Herbie and his friends had just got their dinner. They'd eat it slowly, savoring every bite. They wouldn't be done for hours. When they were, it would be late and they'd go straight home.

Mookie was hungry just watching them.

He jerked his notebook out of his pocket. Who did he have on tonight? Gus, Chico, and Cousin Lou were all there. Paulie would be coming on to overlap Gus, who would be leaving at midnight.

Mookie looked up Paulie's number and gave him a call.

80

Dinner broke up around ten. Herbie declined a ride home, saying he'd rather walk off his meal. It was only a few blocks anyway. He set off in the opposite direction, surreptitiously glancing around him as he went.

Herbie probably wouldn't have spotted Mookie, who was an old hand at surveillance, but Paulie was another story. A driver first and foremost, a bodyguard second, he was as subtle as a bull in a china shop. Herbie spotted his tail within one block. He had such an easy time doing it he kept looking around for someone else, in case Paulie was the rough shadow he was supposed to spot and ditch, while the smooth shadow took over. After a couple of blocks he'd concluded there was no such thing. The guy was just bad.

Herbie walked home. His doorman had been avoiding him ever since the murder, not knowing what to say. Herbie walked up to him and plowed through his apologies. "There's a guy following me. I'm going to walk over to the elevator like I'm going upstairs, but I'm going to duck in the mailroom instead. Go out on the sidewalk like you're looking for a cab, but don't hail one. See if the guy across the street is still watching the building, or if he's walking away. Big guy with a crew cut."

The doorman gulped. "Yes, sir."

He was back thirty seconds later. "The man you described is walking away."

Herbie tipped the doorman fifty bucks and went out the front door.

Paulie was on the far side of Park Avenue. He reached the corner and took a left.

Herbie hurried to the corner and caught the light. He crossed the street and tailed along behind.

Paulie kept going, crossed the street, and went into a garage between Lexington and Third.

There was a cab coming down the block. Herbie stepped out in the street and hailed it.

The cabbie had a five-o'clock shadow and a Brooklyn twang. He half turned in his seat and said, "Where to, buddy?"

"Right here."

"Huh?"

"Pull over and put your blinkers on."

"We're not going anywhere?"

"Yeah, we are, in a minute."

"Where we going?"

"I don't know."

"I gotta put down a destination."

"Put it down when we get there."

"I gotta put it down now."

"Yeah, but we don't know it now, so we put it down when we get there."

A car pulled out of the garage.

"That's him," Herbie said. "Give him a head start and pull out."

"Give him a head start? What is this?"

Herbie slapped a fifty-dollar bill across the back of the seat. "This is fifty dollars. There's another fifty at the other end if you do as I say."

"Is this illegal?"

"No. You have a perfect right to drive where you want."

"But you're following this guy."

"I hope so. If you lose him, you don't get the fifty bucks."

"I'm not sure I wanna do this."

"Okay. Drop me off next to a cabbie who does."

The cabbie gave him a look, but pulled out and started driving.

307

The car was stopped at a light on Second Avenue.

"Stay back. If he spots you, you don't get the fifty bucks. And he'll probably shoot you in the head."

"Are you shitting me?"

"Yeah. I'll still give you the fifty, even if he shoots you in the head."

"I don't wanna do this."

"I'm kidding. It's fine. Here's the other fifty. There's two more at the other end if you get me there and he hasn't spotted us on the way."

The car went over the Fifty-ninth Street Bridge and drove straight to a shabby house in Queens. There was a parking space out front. The guy parked the car and went in.

"Drive on by," Herbie said.

"I need the number."

"No, you don't. You're not writing it down."

The cabbie looked betrayed. "You said I could write down the number."

"You don't need the number. Put down the cross streets. That's what I gave you. The cross streets. Isn't that how you write down most addresses? Fifty-seventh and Seventh?"

"Not outside Manhattan."

"Yeah, well, this time the passenger did.

Drive down to the corner, turn left, and stop. You can write down the cross streets."

"You're paying me off?"

"Yeah. Here's the hundred I promised, plus enough to cover the meter. If you want a return fare, hang out here counting your money. I should be back."

"How long?"

"I don't know. Half an hour."

"Half an hour?"

"Or however long you think another hundred-dollar bonus is worth. Just don't decide to knock on the front door and ask me if I'm going back."

From the terrified look in the cabbie's eyes, there was no danger of that.

81

Herbie hurried down the block to the address. The house had a concrete walkway to the door. He hesitated, afraid of making noise that would alert whoever was inside to his presence. There was a front lawn the size of a postage stamp, but it was thick grass. Herbie walked on it, crept silently up to the door.

There was a front window. The curtains were drawn, but there was a crack at the far right side. An open grate to the basement window just below was a hazard, but Herbie eased around it, leaned close, and peered in.

The man he'd been following was standing in the living room, griping at two men who were sitting at a card table playing cribbage, and a third man just sitting on the couch and watching TV. He didn't seem to be griping about anything in particular, he was the kind of guy who just liked to gripe.

He said something vague about traffic, but there hadn't been any traffic, and something about having to tail a guy first, all of which might have made sense if he were making excuses for being late, only he didn't appear to be late because no one got up to go.

Each one of the guys was sporting a shoulder holster with an ugly-looking gun.

The guy he'd been following said, "So, where's the girl?"

The goon on the couch jerked his thumb. "Upstairs."

"Can I see her?"

"No, you can't see her. What do you think this is, your private peep show? You're here to sit watch."

"What does it matter?"

One of the card players stopped playing long enough to point his finger at the guy. "Because she's important to someone and we don't want to fuck it up. So you pay attention to me. You do not have any contact with the girl. If you do, I'll know, and it will not be good. It will not be, how do they say, conducive to your health."

"Do we get to kill her?"

The player laughed and shook his head. "Fucking idiot. If we gotta kill her, it's not a 'get to' thing, it's a job. And it would be done by the pros, not you. You're just a guy.

311

You got your gun?"

"Yeah."

The guy took it out of his shoulder holster and held it up.

"You don't gotta show us, I'm just asking." To the man on the couch he said, "Jesus, where did you get this dingbat?"

"I didn't get him. Mookie got him."

The card player sighed. "There's one exception," he said.

"What's that?"

"If the cops come, you kill the girl and get out."

82

By the time he got home, Herbie was a nervous wreck. He knew where Melanie was, but he couldn't rescue her. If he went to Dino, the cops would raid the place and those jerks would kill the girl. So what could he do?

He could go into court and throw the case. That would buy some time, but that would destroy his client's life. It could put him in danger, too. In jail, some subhuman specimen could attack him in the shower or stab him during lunch.

Unfortunately, it was the lesser of two evils. David's possible demise, balanced against Melanie's almost certain one. The gunmen he'd seen through the window weren't subtle. They had made their intentions known. At the slightest hint of a rescue the girl was dead. That was the way they played. It might not be what the brains of the outfit wanted, but it was what the menials intended to carry out.

Herbie had to rescue her himself. Pose as a mailman, pose as a cable TV repairman, pose as a pizza delivery boy, for Christ's sakes, he knew that worked, all you needed was a box. He could probably talk his way in, but what did he do then? Overpower three or four armed thugs with his bare hands? The chance of that succeeding seemed awfully slim.

Herbie wished he had a gun. He'd had one for years, got rid of it when he cleaned up his act. The gun had gone the way of everything else. Everything except his IOU. That had survived over the years, despite being paid off, and transferred, and forgotten, and remembered, and transferred again, a worthless piece of paper that might well cost him *his* life.

Why hadn't he ditched the IOU and hung on to his gun?

83

Herbie got up at six, rented a car, and headed for upstate New York. On the way he called Stone Barrington.

"I'm not going to be in court."

"Are you sick?"

"I'm fine. I've just got things to do."

"In the midst of a criminal trial?"

"I know you can handle it."

"Herbie."

"You were going to be there anyway, Stone. What's the big deal?"

"What do you want me to do?"

"Let the witness go."

"You're kidding."

"The jurors are getting bored. Let him go."

"I can't tell if you're serious."

"I'm serious. We've made our point."

"We got an adjournment so he could get his notes."

"Right. I guess we have to ask him about

that. What was he looking up?"

"Herbie."

"Oh. How did they know David would be at the party? I'm sure he's come up with a good answer. Let him tell it and let him go."

"Shouldn't I show a *little* interest in the answer?"

"Why? No one else will. Time to score some points with the jury. Throw it back in the ADA's court. If he wants to ask him questions, there's nothing we can do about that."

A speeder whizzed by on the left.

"Are you in your car?" Stone said.

"No, I got the TV on," Herbie said. Lying to Stone and Dino again was getting to be a habit.

Herbie got off the phone and concentrated on his driving.

It had been a while since he had taken the tactical training course, but Herbie had no problem recognizing the entrance of Strategic Defenses, despite the unobtrusive sign at the side of the driveway. Were it not for that, it might have passed for any gated community. He announced himself and was buzzed in.

The facility was clearly thriving. There were several new buildings Herbie didn't recognize, including gyms, class buildings, barracks, and even a small medical unit with an ambulance parked out front.

It was a sunny day, and men and women were practicing on the front lawn. Some were doing martial arts. Others were working with weapons, usually in pairs, with an unarmed student pitted against an armed one. The pairings were irrespective of age or sex. It was not unusual for a senior citizen to be matched up with a college student.

Josh Hook came out of the main house as Herbie drove up. With his crew cut and chiseled features, Josh resembled nothing more than a marine drill sergeant. Herbie always had to fight the impulse to say "Sir, yes, sir" when speaking to him.

Josh spread his arms and smiled. "So, Herbie, what do you think?"

"I can see why you want to expand."

"Yeah. Everyone's defense crazy these days. I could use another driving track and a rifle range or two."

"You have your own ambulance?"

Josh grinned. "That's mainly for show. People see it, they take care. Injuries have gone down since I bought it. It's a great deterrent."

"I can imagine."

"The last time I spoke to you, you were being shot at. How did that work out?"

317

"Not well."

Herbie told him about Yvette's murder.

Joshua's eyes widened. "Oh, my God! You're 'New York Midtown lawyer'? Oh, for goodness' sakes. I haven't spoken to Mike in days. I was going to call him this weekend. He'd have clued me in. What's the upshot? They thought you did it but they don't now?"

"More or less."

"So what brings you here?"

"I need a gun."

"And you came all the way up here? There's that place in the city where the cops all shop. Why didn't you get one there?"

"Because the cops all shop there. It would get back to Dino."

"Why would that be bad?"

"Same reason you don't announce covert operations on TV. Dino would act, and people would die. And the fact that I had a gun would be moot."

"Is this something I can help you with?"

Herbie considered the offer. Josh would be a valuable ally if he just knew how to use him. "Thanks. I'll let you know. Could you be prepared to move on a moment's notice?"

"Just say the word. You really want a gun?"

"Yeah."

"You'll have to get a carry permit."

"I've got one. *You* got it for me when this place opened and I took your course."

"So you need a gun. I understand you don't want to go to a cop store. But there must be a dozen places in the city you could have got it without driving all the way up here. What's the deal?"

"It been a long time, Josh. I need a lesson."

Joshua Hook nodded. "Okay. Show me what you got."

Herbie didn't have much. Josh started him off on one of the indoor ranges, shooting a short distance at a paper target. He watched while Herbie emptied the magazine, then reeled the target in. There wasn't a single hole in it.

"You're shooting high to the right," Josh said.

"What do I do?"

"Aim low to the left."

Herbie gave him a look.

"Here's the thing," Josh said. "For years you've been a civilian. You haven't gotten in trouble, you haven't fired a gun. But way back when, aren't you the guy who put two shots in the head of Carmine Dattila?"

"Yeah."

"How many shots did you fire?"

"Two."

"You know why? Because you had to. There was something at stake. The fact that you hated the guy didn't hurt, but here's a bully, an aggressive madman who's going to kill you on a whim. So you walk in the door and, bang, bang! It's not aiming, it's not target shooting. It's just like pointing your finger."

Josh gestured to the door. "Okay, let's go outside."

"Why?"

"What you lawyers call a change of venue."

Josh took Herbie to one of the four outdoor shooting ranges.

"Okay, here we go. I'll walk you through the obstacle course. The targets jump out at you. No time to aim."

"Nothing to remember?"

"Just squeeze the trigger. Don't jerk it high right."

"Fuck you."

"That's the spirit. You got the layout? You go alone. Those are real bullets, and I don't want one."

Herbie walked through the course, firing as the targets popped up. Josh hadn't told him to, but he found himself crouching as

320

he went. He came out feeling good.

"How'd I do?"

"Much better. You actually hit some of the targets. You also hit a cop, a nun, and a kid on a bicycle, but nobody's perfect."

"The nun looked suspicious."

"You want to go again?"

Herbie shook his head. "As long as I'm hitting something, I'm fine."

"So now you want a gun?"

"Can you sell me one?"

"No, but I'll give you one."

"Oh?"

"I figure I owe you."

"Why's that?"

"When you took my course, you refused to run. You said there was no reason to make everyone do it just because I could. You said I'd do better treating the students as professionals rather than raw recruits."

"I was a wiseass in those days."

Josh shook his head. "Not at all. Best advice I ever got. So I figure I can give you a gun."

"Okay. Which one do you want to give me?"

"The one in your hand. Stick it in your pants, and you're good to go."

"Are you kidding me?"

"Yeah. I'll give you a hip holster. But

that's your gun."

"Thanks, Josh."

Josh walked Herbie out to the car. Herbie got in and started the engine. Josh rapped on the window. Herbie rolled it down.

"Yeah?"

"Try not to shoot any nuns."

84

Judge Buckingham looked down at the defense table. "Mr. Fisher is not in court?"

"No, Your Honor," Stone said. "Mr. Fisher was unavoidably detained. I will carry on in his absence."

"Very well. Bring in the jury and return the witness to the stand."

When that had been done, Stone Barrington stood and approached the witness.

"Have you consulted your notes, Detective Kelly?"

Kelly looked smug. "Yes, I have."

"And can you tell us who advised you that David Ross would be at the party?"

"No one."

Stone frowned. "No one? Then why were you at the party?"

"I was told there would be *drugs* at the party. I was sent there to make an arrest."

Stone frowned. Herbie had told him to accept the answer and quit, but he couldn't let that statement go unchallenged. "Detective, I have been over the transcript and I am certain that you testified that you were at the party because you were acting on intel that *David Ross* would be there selling drugs. Not just anyone, but David Ross specifically. Do you recall making that statement? We can have the transcript read back, if you need to refresh your memory."

Clearly, Detective Kelly was prepared for the question. He was quite unruffled. "I'll take your word for it," he said magnanimously. "If I made that statement, I was mistaken. The intel was merely that drugs were being sold at the party, and a major source of narcotics would be there. It turned out the major source of narcotics was David Ross, but we didn't know it until we caught him selling drugs."

Stone blinked. The answer to the question had made things ten times worse. A major source of narcotics, indeed. He could object and get most of the answer thrown out on the grounds of being conclusions on the part of the witness and assuming facts not in evidence, but that would just underline the testimony for the jury. It didn't matter if it was in the record. They'd heard it, and the damage was done.

"You were mistaken when you said that

you were acting on intel that David Ross would be selling drugs at the party?"

"That's right."

"You realize you were under oath?"

"I wasn't lying. I misspoke."

"Are you claiming you *accidentally* committed perjury?"

Detective Kelly was unruffled. "It's only perjury if you make a false statement knowing it to be false. When I made that statement I thought it was true. It was only after I was asked to research it that I realized I was mistaken."

Stone smiled. "So you studied up on the laws of perjury. I thought you might have."

"Objection, Your Honor," ADA Grover said.

"Sustained."

"And what other portions of your testimony are you hazy about?"

"Objection."

"Overruled."

"I'm not hazy about any of it. I misremembered one thing I'd been told. I am absolutely certain about what I saw and did."

"Uh-huh," Stone said. "Then I hate to ask you about what you were told, but *who* told you there would be drugs at the party?"

"The duty officer."

"And who would that be?"

"Sergeant O'Hara."

"Sergeant O'Hara told you there would be drugs at the party?"

"That's right."

"How did he know?"

"Objection. Hearsay."

"Sustained."

"No further questions," Stone said, and sat down.

There was a stunned silence in the courtroom. A spectator giggled. A juror nearly applauded.

The witness, clearly prepared with a litany of answers, looked like a student who had crammed all night only to have the teacher cut him off before he could dazzle the girls in class with his knowledge.

Judge Buckingham recovered first. He turned to the prosecutor. "Mr. Grover. Any redirect for this witness?"

The ADA clearly didn't know. He hesitated a moment, suspecting a trap, then said, "No questions, Your Honor."

"The witness is excused," Judge Buckingham said. "Call your next witness."

"The prosecution calls Julie Parker."

Ms. Parker was an attractive young woman dressed in loose-fitting business attire that tended to deemphasize her figure. Dressed as a hip young college student, Stone figured, she would be enticing indeed.

ADA Grover asked a few preliminary questions establishing that she was an undercover narcotics agent, Stone stipulated her qualifications, and they were off to the races.

As the direct examination started, Mookie slipped out and made the call.

Taperelli was not pleased. "That's not good."

"Mr. Fisher is doing what you asked," Mookie said.

"Yeah, but he's not there."

"No, but Stone Barrington is, and he's taking a dive. He let the detective go."

"What's his game?"

"No game. He's throwing in the towel."

"I don't like it."

"What's not to like? It's exactly what you wanted."

"Yeah, but I didn't expect to get it. Not that easily. And we don't know where Mr. Fisher is."

"I wasn't tailing him this morning. There was no need. He had to be in court."

"But he's not there."

"No."

"So there *was* a need."

"Maybe. We don't know why."

"That's why you should have been tailing him like I'd asked. I need to know what he's up to. I have people asking me who want to know why he's not in court. What am I supposed to tell them? That we lost track of him because Mookie didn't think there was a need to keep tabs?"

"So what do you want me to do?"

"Stay in court. If he shows up, let me know. This case needs to be wrapped up today."

85

Dino didn't know there'd been a kidnapping. He was just a man with a murder case to solve.

The David Ross case was another matter entirely. It still looked like a frame-up, engineered by a crooked detective and a mob boss, but it had nothing to do with the murder.

There was also the intimidation and corruption of defense attorney James Glick. Dino had a finger on that pulse, even if it wasn't top priority. James Glick, though a victim, was also an accomplice. If he'd conspired with Tommy Taperelli to thwart justice by fleeing the jurisdiction of the court, the fact that he'd been coerced into such action would be a matter for his attorneys to raise should the case ever come to trial. But Dino had him on the books as a fugitive, and Dino was keeping track. When last sighted, James Glick was headed southwest and would be reaching Texas soon.

Where he went from there was anybody's guess. The man was running scared.

Would bringing him back help Herbie? That was the question. The answer was probably not. He could take over the court case, but right now the court case was the only thing Herbie had to focus on.

The intercom buzzed.

"Yes?" Dino said.

"Stone Barrington on line two."

Dino clicked it on. "Hi, Stone, how's it going?"

"Not great. Herbie didn't show up for court."

"Again? What's he done now?"

"This time he's not arrested. At least I think he isn't. He called, told me he wasn't coming, asked me to carry on."

"Did he say why?"

"He said he was busy."

"Well, that's broad enough to cover everything in the penal code. When did you speak to him?"

"He called on my way to court. He seemed casual enough. It sounded like he was in a car, only he said he wasn't."

"He's lying to us again?"

"Hey, he tried to marry a hooker and got

arrested. Can lying be far behind?"

"Have you tried calling him?"

"It went to voice mail. If I thought it was Taperelli who killed his girlfriend, I'd be scared."

"Could that be why he's ducking the case? I find that hard to believe. He stood up in court and took on the world."

"Until this morning."

"What about this morning?"

"He told me to let Detective Kelly go. We had him on the run. Herbie stumped him with a question, and Kelly asked for an adjournment to consult his notes. Herbie told me to let him report what he found and just quit."

"Did you do that?"

"I did. He's off the stand."

"So the prosecution is done?"

"No, they called a corroborating witness, an undercover agent who was there at the party."

"Would that be a woman?"

"Yes."

"Attractive?"

"She would be in undercover attire."

"Are you going to ask her anything?"

"I might have one or two questions."

"Have fun, Stone. Let me know if Herbie resurfaces."

Dino hung up the phone thinking hard. It didn't add up. Dino could understand Herbie's behavior if Taperelli was leaning on him, if he'd been the one to kill Yvette and was now threatening Herbie. But the evidence pointing to Yvette's killer was clear. They had his fingerprints, his face on videotape, and the identification of the doorman. Plus the corroborating evidence of the prisoner he'd ratted out, who'd picked Yvette's picture out of a lineup.

The intercom buzzed.

"Yes?"

"Detective Brogan to see you."

"Send him in."

Brogan entered, his expression sheepish.

"What's up, Detective?"

"There's something else we overlooked, sir."

Dino smiled. "Are you sure that's how you want to lead off, Detective?"

"Yeah, it is. Because it's true, and I should take responsibility."

"Just what are you taking responsibility for?"

"The surveillance video in the building."

"We have the video of the perpetrator delivering the pizza."

"Yes, sir. That's not the video I'm referring to. You see, no one paid too much at-

332

tention to the surveillance video because initially the suspect was discovered at the scene of the crime with the murder weapon in his hand. And when the second suspect emerged, he could be seen quite clearly in the video from the lobby camera, as well as the camera in the elevator, in which he could be seen both going up to and down from the apartment. So there was little reason to look for anyone else."

"Such as?"

"It turns out there's no video from the back staircase on the night of the murder. That in itself is no big deal. The cameras were on a circuit, and that circuit was out. But there's video from the day before. Those cameras all went out just before the suspect went up with the pizza."

"Why would he put the cameras out and then take the elevator?"

"Clearly he wouldn't. Which brings up the possibility of another perpetrator."

Dino grinned. "Are you trying to get back at me for pointing out the evidence of the robbery?"

The detective flushed. "No, sir. Like I said, I'm pointing out another area in which I was deficient."

"I'm kidding, Detective. This is excellent work, and I appreciate you bringing it to me. Are you saying with the cameras out it would have been possible for someone to get in and out of the building without being seen?"

"Yes, sir. There's cameras in the elevators and main stairwells, but not in the penthouse hallway. If someone got into the back stairway, they could have gone right into the apartment without being seen."

"It's a theory, but it's just a theory."

"It's more than that. The cameras didn't just go out. Someone cut the feed. The feed was cut in the garage, from which there's also access to the back stairwell. If someone got into the garage and took out the cameras, they could go right up and no one would know."

"Could they get into the garage without being seen?"

"Yes, sir, I checked it out. The cameras are aimed at the cars. A person on foot could get in hugging the wall and avoid the cameras all the way back to where the wire was cut."

"What's to stop someone from doing that?"

"The attendant. It's a manned garage. The attendant at the entrance would stop anyone on foot."

"How many attendants?"

"Just one. It's a private garage, for the tenants in the building. He's not renting space, he's just there to wave off cars that don't belong."

Dino frowned. "Interesting."

"Anyway, I thought you should know."

"You thought right, Detective. Who knows about this?"

"No one. I reported directly to you."

"Anything you get, report directly to me. Let's keep this from the media if we can."

"Yes, sir."

"Now that we know what we're looking for, are there any video cameras on the street that would show the entrance to that garage?"

"Apparently there are two. Neither is from a great angle. One is across the street and down the block. The other is on the same side as the garage and shooting diagonally across. It would show people approaching the garage, but not going in. I have detectives reviewing the footage from the day of the murder now."

"Good. As soon as you get something, let me know."

Dino sat at his desk, thinking. What the detective had told him put a whole new spin on everything. It was possible that someone other than the sneak thief had been at Herbie's apartment that night. And just like that, Tommy Taperelli was back in the mix.

Could Tommy Taperelli's boys have killed Yvette? If that were true, things might suddenly make sense. It could explain why Herbie had been acting so strange lately, telling Stone not to cross-examine the witness.

Could Tommy Taperelli be putting the pressure on Herbie? He'd put the pressure on James Glick so badly he'd run. At least, that was the supposition. If that were true, it would go a long way toward proving he was doing the same to Herbie. And that he'd possibly killed Yvette Walker.

Dino snatched up the phone and called the officer he'd put in charge of tracing James Glick. "Carlson, it's Dino. Where was our runaway lawyer last spotted?"

Tommy Taperelli was also monitoring James Glick's movements. People didn't run out on Tommy Taperelli and live to tell of it. Tommy Taperelli had his own national network, perhaps not as extensive as Dino's, but every bit as effective. And Tommy Taperelli's boys actually had a big advantage over Dino's. They didn't have to bother about warrants, or extradition. They didn't have to bother about Miranda, or habeas corpus, or probable cause. They only had to bother about not getting caught. Otherwise, as soon as they found James Glick, they were done.

So was he.

86

James Glick spotted them from the glass elevator he was riding down from his tenth-floor room in the Hyatt Regency. They were at the front desk checking the registration. At least that's what it looked like. One guy was distracting the desk clerk while the other was surreptitiously checking out the register. He could swear the guy was leaning over the counter to look at the computer screen.

And there he was, in a glass elevator, heading right into their arms.

He flailed out his hand, pressed a floor at random. Mezzanine. That was good. Anything that wasn't Lobby.

He got off the elevator and leaned over the mezzanine balcony to get a closer look.

These guys were different. They didn't look like the guys he had been mistaking for goons ever since he got on the Amtrak express. These were the real thing. They looked tough, mean, and they carried themselves differently, with the effortless authority that came with power.

And they didn't have suitcases. A dead giveaway. He'd realized that after getting a few funny looks himself. After that he'd bought a carry-on suitcase to blend in. But these guys clearly didn't care.

James Glick knew he was just being stupid. It was the same thing all over again. These guys would turn out to be businessmen there for a convention. They'd left their suitcases in their car while they checked in. And they wouldn't take the elevator to the tenth floor to check on him, they'd get off on six, where they were staying.

He watched them get into the glass elevator and tried to tell himself it was just his imagination. Then one guy stooped to tie his shoe, and his jacket fell open, revealing his shoulder holster.

James Glick shrank back in horror. As soon as the elevator passed the mezzanine, he ran to it and watched the floor indicator. Sure enough, they got off at the tenth floor.

James Glick was breathing hard. There was an exit door at the end of the corridor. He pushed it open, thundered down a flight of stairs, ran out the door of the Hyatt, and hailed a cab.

87

Herbie called Stone on his way back from
Strategic Defenses.

"What's going on?"

"They broke for lunch."

"How did it go with the detective?"

"Fine. He's off the stand."

"What did he say?"

"He said no one told him David would be
at the party, he heard drugs were being sold
there, and when he checked it out the
person selling them was David."

"What did you do?"

"I challenged him with his previous testimony, got him to admit he was mistaken,
and asked him what *other* portions of his
testimony he was unsure of."

"I told you to let him go."

"I let him go. I just didn't do it with a pat
on the back."

"Okay. Fine."

"Why did you ask him the question in the

first place?"

"Oh. Well, he's framing my client, so he's lying about everything. And he's not too careful about it, because Taperelli's pulling the strings and the case is a slam-dunk. So I went over the transcript to see if he had made any stupid mistakes. Sure enough, right off the bat he says he was acting on intel David Ross was selling drugs at the party, which is total bullshit. No one told him David was at the party. He probably didn't even know about the party. In all likelihood he was following David around looking for a place to set him up. The party seemed like a good bet. So who told him David Ross would be at the party is a tough question to answer, because nobody did."

"That's good reasoning. You present your case that well to the jury, you just might get your client off."

"Fuck you, too, Stone."

"I get your logic. I mean why did you ask the question if you don't care about the answer?"

"I asked the question to shake him up. Who told him David would be at the party? Well, he's either got to name someone else who is in on the conspiracy, which is nice to know, or he has to admit he made a mistake."

"He opted for the mistake. I would have liked to exploit it."

"You did fine."

A car went by.

"Are you still watching TV?"

"Yes. So where are we now?"

"The prosecution called a corroborating witness, an undercover officer who was at the party."

"Good. Don't ask her anything. Just let her go."

"Herbie, what's going on? Are you giving up on the case?"

"Not at all. We've been going about it all wrong. The jury's heard nothing for days but that detective saying David Ross is a druggie. Now we've got another detective who's going to say the same thing. It's giving the prosecution the advantage. We've got to stop playing defense."

"I get the strategy, but I've got to ask her something so it doesn't look like we've thrown in the towel."

"Okay. Ask her about the arrest. When the detective told David to empty his pockets, did David reach in and get the envelope, or did the detective take it out of his pocket? That will tell us if she's part of the frame-up. If she says David got it, she's clean. If she insists the detective took it out of his pocket, she's in on it, and she's parroting the talking points."

"How do you figure that?"

"I thought you read the transcript. It's in there."

"Don't piss me off, Herbie. What's actually going on?"

"Relax. I'll try to make it."

Herbie clicked the phone off and stepped on the gas.

88

Detective Brogan called Dino back. "We got it!"

"Oh?"

"It's only the camera across the street, and it's not from a great angle, but you can see two men entering the garage on foot shortly before eight o'clock on the night of the murder."

"Can you identify them?"

"No. Like I said, it's a bad angle. You don't get a shot of their faces. But they're big guys, and they look like thugs. And as far as we can tell, they snuck in."

"How do you figure?"

"They waited until the attendant was down the block. Somehow they distracted his attention. I don't know how, but there's video of him coming out of the garage and hurrying down the block. Right after that the two guys come from the opposite direction and enter the garage hugging the wall,

344

just like a guy would have to do to avoid the video cameras."

"Can you send me the video?"

"I'm on it. But you're going to see what I see. The back of two guys' heads. Nothing distinctive about them, except they're two big, solid guys. Dark, nondistinctive clothing. Nothing much to make an ID."

"They're the only ones who entered the garage?"

"They're the only ones who entered the garage on foot. Anyone could have driven in."

"Did any cars drive in while the attendant was down the street?"

"No. It was only a minute. The guys went in, the attendant came back. He didn't miss them by much, but he missed them. Aside from that, cars went in and out, but they belong to people who live in the building because the attendant knew them."

"Okay. Send me the video."

"You want to see it now? I'll share it with you in Dropbox."

Dino had barely hung up the phone when his e-mail beeped. It was a message from Detective Brogan (via Dropbox). Dino clicked on it and got a blue rectangle inviting him to View File. He clicked on that and got the video.

Brogan was right. There was no way to tell who the guys were, but they looked like thugs, and they looked like they were sneaking into the garage.

Dino sat back in his chair and scowled.

Much as he hated to admit it, it was looking more and more like Taperelli had Yvette killed.

89

Herbie got back to Manhattan, returned the rental car, stopped by his apartment to drop off the gun, and took a cab to court. He ran down the corridor and came striding through the door to find the jurors in place, the undercover policewoman on the stand, and Judge Buckingham in the process of inquiring whether the prosecuting attorney was ready to resume questioning.

The judge broke off and held up his hand. "One moment, Mr. Prosecutor. I see the other defense attorney has decided to grace us with his presence. Mr. Fisher, did you forget what time court convenes?"

"I'm sorry, Your Honor," Herbie said. "I'm ready to go. Don't let me hold you up."

"I'm afraid it's a little late for that. Ladies and gentlemen, stay where you are. If you would indulge me for a few minutes. Mr. Fisher, in my chambers, if you please."

Judge Buckingham turned and stalked off. Herbie had to run to catch up.

As soon as the chambers door closed behind them, Judge Buckingham rounded on Herbie. "Mr. Fisher, when you started these shenanigans I looked you up."

Uh-oh.

"It would appear you have been in my courtroom before. The reason I didn't remember you is it was not as an attorney. You appeared for disturbing the peace, resisting arrest, and assaulting a policeman."

"Your Honor, I fail to see that my police record has any bearing on these proceedings."

"It does not. Only it would appear to explain your utter disdain for the law. It's seldom that an attorney has appeared in my court with such an adversarial attitude, not just toward his opponent but toward the judge himself. I did not understand your personal animosity until your record came to light. Perhaps it explains why almost every aspect of your presentation borders on contempt of court."

"That was not my intention, Your Honor. I must say I find this warning irregular at the very least."

"It's not a warning, Mr. Fisher. I thought it only fair to let you know that I have become aware of the fact that we have a history."

"Well, I'm sure that it won't color your judgment any more than it will color mine."

Judge Buckingham's eyes narrowed. "Your remark borders on insolence."

"That's a bad sign. I was trying to show respect."

"I'm in no mood for joking, Mr. Fisher. If I thought your unorthodox behavior was in any way precipitated by our past history, I would take a dim view."

"I understand, Your Honor. Say no more. Believe me, I am as eager as you are to conclude this trial."

Herbie smiled and gestured to the door. "Shall we?"

As they resumed their positions in the court, Stone Barrington whispered, "What was that all about?"

"He doesn't like my attitude."

"Who does?" Stone said.

Judge Buckingham gaveled court to order. "Court is in session. The witness is on the stand. Mr. Prosecutor, do you have any further questions for this witness?"

"No, Your Honor." Grover turned to the defense table. "Your witness."

Stone Barrington started to get to his feet,

but Herbie stopped him. "I've got it."

"Are you sure?"

"Oh, yes."

Herbie approached the witness. It was the first time he'd gotten a good look at her. Julie Parker, despite her youth, appeared to be an experienced and competent undercover detective.

"Ms. Parker, when did you first become aware of the defendant?"

"Detective Kelly pointed him out."

"By name?"

"No, as the man he'd observed selling drugs. He told me to check him out."

"What did that entail?"

"I was to get next to him, bump into him, apologize, and smile. The usual."

"Let me ask you this. Were you there when Detective Kelly searched the defendant?"

"Yes, I was."

"And did he remove an envelope from the defendant's pocket?"

Parker shook her head. "He did not. The *defendant* reached in his pocket and took out that envelope."

"Thank you. And you say Detective Kelly pointed the defendant out to you?"

"That's right."

"How long had you been at the party before he did so?"

"It was right after I arrived."

"You weren't there, staking out the party?"

"No. Detective Kelly called for backup."

"So when you showed up, he had already spotted the defendant?"

"That's right."

"Did you witness any of the transactions Detective Kelly testified to? When the defendant and other students left the room?"

"No. I was just there for the bust."

"Thank you. No further questions."

The witness was stunned.

So was the judge. It took him a second to recover. "Any redirect, Mr. Grover?"

The prosecutor was also caught off guard. "Ah, no, Your Honor."

"The witness is excused. Call your next witness."

"Yes, Your Honor. If you will forgive me, I had expected cross-examination to take all afternoon."

"Clearly, it didn't," Judge Buckingham said dryly. "Call your next witness."

"Yes, Your Honor. The prosecution calls Felix Weintraub."

No one came forward.

Grover glanced around nervously. "Ah, if I might have a brief recess. I believe he's in the building."

"Then find him. We'll wait."

ADA Grover dispatched a law clerk to fetch the witness. As the young man hurried up the aisle, Stone leaned over to whisper to Herbie, "Why didn't you follow up with the lady cop?"

"I got what I wanted. She isn't part of the frame-up. She's cleared on several counts. She contradicts what Detective Kelly said about taking the envelope out of David's pocket, she didn't see any of the alleged transactions, and she doesn't claim she was staking out the party."

A bald, bespectacled man bustled through the back door and down the aisle.

ADA Grover's face broke into a relieved smile. "Here's Mr. Weintraub now, Your Honor."

"Very well. Proceed."

Felix Weintraub qualified himself as a fingerprint expert, and testified to finding the defendant's fingerprints on the envelope containing the packets of cocaine.

When it was his turn, Herbie asked, "Did you find anyone else's fingerprints *besides* the defendant's on that envelope?"

"No. Just his."

"That's all."

Grover called the chemist, for the quantitative analysis of the cocaine in the envelope.

Again, Herbie asked only the most perfunctory questions.

ADA Grover, having ripped through his case in record time, asked for a recess to decide if he wanted to put forth more evidence or rest his case.

Judge Buckingham was scowling as he left the bench.

90

Stone called Dino during recess.

"Herbie's in court."

"How does he seem? Like last night?"

"Sort of."

"What do you mean, 'sort of'?"

"If I didn't know better, I'd think he spent the morning with a therapist. God knows he could use it."

"Is he ripping into the witnesses again, or is he letting you handle them?"

"Neither one. He's insisting on taking the witnesses, and he's giving them the lightest cross-examination you ever heard. He asked the undercover cop what she was told to do. She testified to bumping into David, apologizing, and smiling at him. And he didn't even ask a follow-up."

"I imagine you'd have had some further questions."

"Herbie didn't. He let her go. He asked the fingerprint expert a couple of questions establishing that David's fingerprints were on the contraband, and left it at that."

"You're kidding."

"No. And when the chemist testified as to the purity of the cocaine, Herbie asked him if it was pretty good shit."

"He didn't."

"Well, he didn't use the word *shit,* but it was in that vein. I tell you, Herbie did a better job of making the prosecution's case than they did."

"You think Taperelli threatened him?"

"He's certainly acting like it."

"I bet that's it. There's a chance Taperelli's men killed Yvette after all."

"What? How is that possible?"

"The surveillance cameras in the back stairwell were out that night. Someone cut the feed to the whole circuit just before the murder. It was cut in the garage, and, apparently, it's possible to get into the garage on foot without appearing on camera."

"Is there any way to tell if anybody did?"

"We have surveillance video of two men entering the garage on foot shortly before eight o'clock on the night of the murder."

"Can you identify them?"

"No, the angle's bad. But they look big, like thugs, and they appear to be sneaking in. It's clear from their posture they don't belong."

"What about the boyfriend, Dressler?"

"He might have come along after, found her dead, and robbed the place. It makes more sense than him killing his accomplice while she was still setting up the sting."

"You think Taperelli killed Yvette, Herbie knows it, and that's why he's throwing the trial?"

"I don't know, but I mean to find out. If that's the case, Herbie could be in a lot of trouble."

"How do you want to handle it?"

"I'm going to put a man on Herbie. Just because he's doing what they told him doesn't mean he's safe."

"I'll feel better if you do. Something's going on."

When they returned from recess, ADA Grover announced that after due consideration, the prosecution was resting their case.

"Very well," Judge Buckingham said. "The defense will put on theirs. It's a little late in the day to begin, but we have made good progress today, so let's adjourn until ten o'clock tomorrow morning. Jurors are reminded once again not to talk about the case. Mr. Fisher, please see me in chambers. Court is adjourned."

"What's up?" Stone said.

"He probably wants to congratulate me on my handling of the case."

"You want me to wait? Grab some dinner?"

Herbie shook his head. "I'm beat. I'm going straight home. I'll probably order takeout."

Stone was glad to hear it. If Herbie stayed home, he'd be safe, and the man Dino had tailing him would have an easy time of it.

"Listen. I got a call from Dino. It turns out the surveillance cameras in the back stairwell of your building were out on the night of the murder. Anyone could have gotten in or out unseen from the garage. So it wasn't necessarily the boyfriend. It might have been Taperelli's men after all."

Herbie's jaw was set. "Is that right?"

"There's video from a street camera of two thugs sneaking into the garage."

Herbie took a deep breath and blew it out again.

"I don't mean to upset you, but I thought you should know."

"Dino's been keeping this from me?"

"Don't blame Dino. He just found out. Look, Herbie, don't get any ideas about Taperelli. These guys play in a different league."

"You were going to tell me this over dinner?"

Stone smiled. "It seems like we always give you bad news over dinner, doesn't it?"

"Thanks, Stone. Well, I mustn't keep the judge waiting."

Herbie found Judge Buckingham in chambers. He was leaning back in his desk chair with his hands folded in his lap. His fingers were intertwined, and he was tapping his two thumbs together.

"Yes, Your Honor?"

The judge cocked his head. "I noticed a distinct change in your strategy this afternoon."

"I beg your pardon?"

"Do you have anything to say for yourself?"

Herbie felt like a student who'd been summoned to the principal's office. "I don't know what you want me to say. I find your asking the question somewhat irregular."

"Oh, do you now? We are off the record, Mr. Fisher. You may speak candidly."

"I have no idea why I am here."

"Then you're being disingenuous. Your behavior in court this afternoon was exemplary. You were the very model of speed and efficiency. You asked only pertinent questions, and few of those. None were objectionable on any grounds whatsoever. You were polite, courteous, and cooperative."

"Thank you, Your Honor."

"This is in sharp contrast to your performance during the rest of the trial. A complete one-eighty. It occurs to me a desperate attorney might point to our conversation before court and claim it had intimidated him into curtailing his cross-examination."

"It's a good thing I'm not desperate, Your Honor, or I would think you were talking about me."

Judge Buckingham raised his finger. "See, now that sounds more like the smart aleck I've grown used to."

Herbie sighed. Some days you just couldn't win. "Your Honor, if a lawyer had done what you've just implied I've done, I would think it would be a matter for the Bar Association."

Judge Buckingham's eyes narrowed. "To consider a charge of intimidation?"

"Certainly not. To consider the lawyer's attempt to pervert justice. It's a good thing neither of us is contemplating such an action."

Judge Buckingham looked buffaloed. He clearly wanted to say something, but Herbie's attitude had left him speechless.

"Well, if there's nothing else, Your Honor,

I have to prepare for the case. The defense is up tomorrow."

Herbie bowed and nodded his way out the door, leaving the judge utterly frustrated.

91

Herbie spotted Dino's man as he was getting onto the subway. He'd tried to get a taxi, but it was rush hour, so there were no cabs to be had, so he'd walked down to City Hall to catch the Lexington Avenue express.

Herbie spotted him getting onto the car. At first he thought he was one of Taperelli's men. Or, rather, one of Detective Kelly's men. Herbie could tell from the man's unmistakable bearing that he was a cop — he just didn't know if he was a good cop or a bad cop. He was an undercover cop, perhaps out of Kelly's stable.

The guy wasn't a bad tail. Herbie only spotted him because he couldn't get on the car until Herbie did, and in the rush-hour crunch, there was no room and the conductor was trying to close the door on him. The loudspeaker was squawking, "There's a train right behind us! Let the doors go!" in a distorted, tinny voice. Then he noticed a man trying to get onto the car at all costs, and it dawned on him he was a cop.

The cop followed Herbie all the way back to his apartment. Herbie noticed him a few times, but only because he'd already spotted him in the subway car. Otherwise, he wouldn't have had a clue.

Herbie went into the bar, poured himself a shot of Knob Creek, tossed it off, and collapsed on the couch in a heap.

All right, what the hell did he do now?

The cop was a problem. Taking on Taperelli's men alone wouldn't be easy, and the cop added an unnecessary complication. If the cop followed him to the hideout in Queens, he'd come crashing in as soon as he realized what was going on. But he'd be too little too late. Herbie'd probably be dead by the time he reached the door.

Herbie's cell phone rang. He pulled it out, checked caller ID.

He groaned. It was Mario Payday.

He'd forgotten all about Mario Payday. The guy wanted ninety thousand bucks or he'd kill him. Well, he'd just have to wait in line. Herbie sent the call to voice mail. He wondered if Mario would leave a message or if such tactics were beneath him.

Herbie considered calling Joshua Hook at Strategic Defenses. He should have taken him up on his offer to help. Was it too late now? Josh could be here in, what, an hour and forty-five minutes? But what would he be? Just another person to pique the interest of the police escort. If Dino heard Josh was here, he'd throw every cop in the area in the mix.

Herbie's phone beeped.

Mario Payday had finished leaving his voice mail message. Herbie clicked it on and played it back.

"Mr. Fisher, this is Carlo, Mario Payday's assistant. I'm calling because Mario does not like to make this sort of call himself. Which I quite understand. I'm calling because you have not paid Mario yet. Which I *don't* understand. A man such as you should have the wherewithal and the perspicacity — don't ask me, Mario told me to use the word — to discharge the debt before it becomes an issue. If you do not discharge it this evening, Mr. Fisher, Mario will be forced to cut his losses and make an example out of you, as a lesson to other debtors who might come to think that a financial obligation is something to be taken lightly.

"Mario will be sad to lose you. He finds you amusing."

Herbie slipped the phone back in his pocket.

92

David knew something was wrong. His father had been acting strange all day. For the last two days, actually, ever since he'd come and pulled Herbie away from lunch. David didn't like it. He was the one on trial. He was the one in danger. And now his own father and lawyer were keeping things from him. It was like he had no one to trust. A hell of a position for a college-age kid, already feeling like he was up against the world.

David finished his dinner, which he'd eaten alone in the big dining room, thinking he should have gotten a TV tray in his own room, only he'd hoped his father would join him for the meal. He didn't.

David went to check on the councilman. The door to his father's study was closed, which meant he desired privacy.

David pushed the door open and went in. The councilman was slumped in his chair.

A bottle of whiskey was open on the desk in front of him. He was a man on the brink of despair.

"Dad, what's wrong?"

Councilman Ross immediately straightened in his chair. "It's nothing. Just business problems."

"Bullshit."

"David."

"Dad, I don't know what's going on, but it's not just me. I've been on trial for days. I didn't do it, but you're overreacting even if I did. And I'm not going to leave you alone until you tell me why."

The councilman looked at his son standing in front of him, strong and determined. He sighed and all the resistance oozed out of him.

"It's your sister."

93

Herbie didn't know what to do. The whole world was crashing down on him. The cops were after him. The mobsters were after him. Now a loan shark was after him. And he didn't have time for any of them, not if he was going to rescue Melanie Porter.

The thought was amusing. Rescuing the girl. What was he, the hero in some adventure story? No, he was just Herbie Fisher, attorney-at-law, and, sadly enough, the best chance Melanie Porter had.

He had to get out of his apartment building without being seen. Could it be done? Dino had advanced the theory that Taperelli's men could have gotten in because they'd cut the cameras for the stairwell. Presumably he could go down those stairs. But what difference would it make? The cop wouldn't be watching the security cameras. Herbie was a tenant. Nobody gave a damn if he used the elevator.

The stairwell led to the garage, presumably the method of egress used by Taperelli's men. Well, the elevator did, too. He could take the elevator down to the garage. He didn't have a car, but he could just walk out the entrance. The garage man didn't know him, but he wouldn't stop him going *out*.

Of course, if the cop was worth his salt, he would have made note of the garage entrance and taken up a position on the corner diagonally across from the building from which he could watch the main entrance and the garage entrance at the same time.

He didn't dare risk it. He only had one shot, and if he guessed wrong, it could mean Melanie's life.

Herbie paced up and down. Think, damn it, think. You don't have to do this alone. Swallow your pride.

Herbie smiled slightly.

He snatched up his cell phone, punched in a number. "Josh? It's Herbie."

Joshua Hook chuckled. "Don't tell me. You shot somebody, and the cops will be tracking the gun."

"This morning you offered to help. Does that offer still stand?"

"What do you need?"

"How quick can you get to Manhattan?"

"Pretty damn quick. I'm there now."

"What?"

"I had some business in town this afternoon. I'm about to have dinner."

"Mind postponing it a little?"

"What do you need?"

94

Joshua Hook frowned at Herbie skeptically. "You're being followed by a thug?"

"Yes."

"Over an old gambling debt?"

"Back before I was a lawyer."

"A debt you've already paid off?"

"That's the crazy thing."

"That's *one* of the crazy things. This whole thing is crazy."

"Maybe so, but the guy is out there."

"All right. You say you've paid the debt off?"

"Yes."

"Have you considered paying it off *again*?"

Herbie frowned. "What?"

"If this is causing you as much trouble as you claim, wouldn't your peace of mind be something worth buying?"

Herbie pretended to consider the idea. "I suppose."

Josh studied his face. "What's the real story?"

"Huh?"

"Come on, Herbie. You drive all the way up to my facility, take a lesson, and get a gun. I can't believe you did that rather than pay someone some money. I mean, we're not talking a hundred thousand here, are we?"

"Ninety."

Josh shook his head. "Did anyone ever teach you moderation?"

"Hey."

"But even so, you won a fortune in the lottery and you're a partner in a law firm. Why are you sweating the small stuff?"

Herbie put up his hands. "All right, all right. It's not the loan shark. It's Tommy Taperelli."

Josh's mouth fell open. "You're mixed up with the mob?"

"I'm not mixed up with the mob. I got roped into handling a criminal case, a drug bust. The defendant got set up by the guys who busted him, and it looks like Taperelli's pulling the strings. He wants me to cease and desist."

"You think that's Taperelli's man on the corner?"

"Probably."

"And you were going to let me walk right into it thinking he works for a loan shark?"

"I know you can take care of yourself."

"Yeah, unless I'm lulled into thinking I'm dealing with an amateur and get coldcocked by a pro."

"I'd still bet on you."

"Thanks a heap. Assuming you get free of this guy, what are you going to do?"

"I'm going to try to get myself out of trouble."

"What sort of trouble are you in?"

"Well, I've been arrested for murder and charged with contempt of court. That's for starters. I also happen to have some witnesses I'd like to talk to without leading Taperelli to them."

Josh sighed. "All right, kid. Let's go take on the mob."

95

Josh had no problem spotting the thug. He was diagonally across Park Avenue from the corner of Herbie's building, right where he could watch the entrance and the garage at the same time. The guy was clearly a pro. There was no way he was just the enforcer for some two-bit loan shark. He was Taperelli's man for sure.

And Herbie hadn't wanted to tell him. That bothered Josh. Did Herbie think he was getting old? Slow? Losing it? Or did he just think Taperelli's men were that scary? Herbie had been dealing with them, and clearly they'd scared him, enough to drive all the way upstate to get a gun. Well, no matter. He'd agreed to do it, so he'd do it.

And Josh was that good. He just needed to be careful, but effective. Come right at the guy. Taunt him. Get him off balance.

Josh walked up to the thug and said, "Hey, asshole, what do you think you're doing?"

The guy ignored him, pretended not to hear.

"Hey, asshole, I'm talking to you," Josh said.

The thug turned then, assessed him calmly. "Run along, buddy."

"No, *you* run along. I like this corner. You've had it long enough."

"I'm glad to hear that because it was getting boring," the thug said, and turned away to continue his surveillance.

"Hey!" Josh said.

The thug turned back. "What?"

"You going to leave this corner?"

The thug stared him down. "No."

Josh punched him in the face.

The blow caught him by surprise. He went down to one knee. He reached for his gun. Josh grabbed his arm, pulled it up behind him until something cracked.

He howled in pain and lashed out with his left hand. He caught Josh just above the left eye and raised a welt. Josh might not have noticed. He cocked his fist.

The thug's arm wasn't broken. He managed a punch to Josh's stomach that took some of the joy out of life. Josh grabbed him by the jacket lapels, dropped to the ground, and rolled over backward, flipping him over his head. He turned around and dove on him before he could scramble to his feet.

A police car with its siren and lights on made a U-turn on Park Avenue and careened to a stop beside them. A second police car took the shorter route against the traffic and screeched to a stop head-to-head with the first. Policemen jumped out of the cars and descended on the combatants. Two grabbed Josh. Two grabbed the thug. They wrestled them toward the cars.

One of the officers holding the thug said, "Hey, this one's armed!"

"I'm a cop, you moron!"

"Yeah, right," the officer scoffed. He threw him into the back of the car.

The other officers had a harder time dealing with Josh Hook. He managed to keep his feet until he saw Herbie, completely forgotten, come out the front door of his apartment building and walk off down the street.

96

David Ross's cab pulled up at the corner of Herbie's building. There was some sort of fracas going on across the street. Two police cars with lights flashing were blocking one lane, and passersby were gawking.

As David was paying off the cab Herbie Fisher came out the door of his apartment building and walked quickly down the street in the opposite direction.

David was tempted to jump out of the car and run after him, but some instinct told him that would be a bad idea. In a flash, David realized what it was. Herbie hadn't paid any attention to the fight going on across the street. It was only normal to stop and watch, at least to see what was going on. Everyone else was. But Herbie hadn't done that. It was almost as if Herbie had known what was going on.

What was Herbie up to?

As far as David knew, Herbie and his

father were the only ones who knew his sister had been kidnapped. Herbie hadn't told the cops, though he had high-placed friends on the force. And Herbie hadn't told his father what he was up to. He was playing a lone game, and he wasn't about to let David in on it. If David stopped him, all it would do would be inhibit the play.

"Hang on," David said to the cabbie, "we're going somewhere else."

97

Herbie was nervous riding along in the cab. He had one shot, and one shot only. He'd gotten out of his apartment building, but that was the least of it. One cop was a lot easier to distract than a bunch of armed thugs, and he'd had help. Well, there was no harm in asking for help. Herbie wasn't trying to prove anything. If someone else did it for him, that was fine with him.

Herbie felt bad about tricking Josh. He'd have to make it up to him, assuming he ever got out of this. He'd bail him out, pay his fine, try to make Dino understand that Josh wasn't in on it at all. Herbie'd completely finessed him, feeding him the story about the loan shark, knowing it wasn't going to fly, then reluctantly admitting the guy was Taperelli's. If he'd led with that, Josh would have been suspicious. As it was, he didn't have a clue. He probably still thought the guy was a hood. Well, whatever the case,

Josh had done a great job.

Unfortunately, there was no one he could call on for the next part of his mission. He and he alone had a shot to save Melanie.

The cab pulled up on the corner of Seventh Avenue and Thirtieth Street. Herbie paid the driver and got out. The downstairs door was open. Herbie went in and rang for the elevator. The car came, an ancient one with buttons that stuck. He pushed eight and rumbled up to the eighth floor.

Herbie strode down the hallway and banged on the frosted glass door with the sign saying FINANCIAL PLANNER.

Carlo flung it open. He gawked when he saw who it was. "What the hell do you want?"

"I need to see your boss."

"About what?"

"None of your fucking business."

That was the right answer. Carlo stepped aside and let Herbie into the office.

Herbie's heart was pounding. He had his gun on his hip, loosely covered by his sports jacket. He'd bullied Carlo to avoid a pat-down, and it had worked. Now if he could just carry it through.

Mario Payday sat behind his desk. Ollie the Ox and another big goon stood on either side of him.

Herbie walked up to Mario, spread his arms wide, and grinned. "It's Payday."

98

When he got the call, Dino Bacchetti came out of his chair. "You arrested *who*!?"

Ten minutes later the guard at the lockup let a rather sheepish-looking detective out of the cell.

"What the hell happened?" Dino said.

"Some guy attacked me for no reason."

"You couldn't handle him?"

"He sucker-punched me, and he knew what he was doing."

"Why did he attack you? Was he drunk?"

"That's how he acted, but I'd bet he was stone-cold sober. He hit me, and it was all I could do to respond. The next thing I know I'm in the back of a police car."

"What was he like?"

"He looked like a marine sergeant, right down to the crew cut and square jaw."

Dino turned to the officer accompanying him. "Let me see the arrest report."

Dino looked at the report. He flipped a

sheet. His eyes widened. "Damn it to hell!"

Joshua Hook was sitting on a cot, his face marred by a black eye and a bloody lip.

"Why'd you beat up my officer?"

"What officer?"

"You beat up the officer I had tailing Herbie Fisher."

"That was a cop?"

"Who the hell did you think it was?"

Josh shrugged. "He looked like a thug."

"You knew he was a cop. That's why you did it. Would it surprise you to know the doorman observed Herbie Fisher leaving his apartment building at approximately the time the fight started?"

"They told me I don't have to say anything until I see my lawyer. Are you him?"

"All right, don't tell me, I'll tell you. The cop was tailing Herbie for his own protection. Herbie always seems to pick a fight with the wrong people. This time he picked a fight with Tommy Taperelli, and Tommy Taperelli is not unresourceful, and Tommy Taperelli doesn't play nice. Now, I don't know what story Herbie told you about the guy, but there's a good chance it was Tommy Taperelli who killed his girlfriend."

"This wasn't about a drug bust?"

Dino sighed. "It is and it isn't. Look, Josh, anything Herbie told you about a drug bust is probably true. I'm guessing he didn't tell you Taperelli probably killed his fiancée."

"I thought it was a burglar."

"So did we. But it might have been Taperelli. We just found out, but I think Herbie suspected all along. Since Herbie found out Taperelli may be behind it, he's come unglued. I don't know what he's contemplating but it can't be good."

Josh frowned.

Dino sighed. "Look, Josh, I'm not just a good friend of Herbie, I happen to be a good friend of Mike Freeman, the founder and CEO of your parent company, Strategic Services, and Mike also happens to be a good friend of Herbie — in fact, Mike was the guy who hired Herbie to work with you in the first place. If I have to get Mike down here, I will, but I don't really have the time. So if you know anything, anything at all that can help me deal with the situation, since thanks to you I have totally lost all contact with Herbie Fisher, you'd better tell me now."

Dino called Stone. "Herbie got away."

"What? How?"

"Herbie got Josh Hook of Strategic Defenses to beat up my detective. He also got him to give him a gun. That's where he was this morning, at the upstate training facility brushing up on his shooting."

"Josh beat up a cop?"

"He thought he was one of Taperelli's men."

"Why did he think that?"

"Herbie sold him on the idea. I don't know how, but he did."

"I can't believe Herbie spotted your man. Your men are good."

"Yeah, but Herbie's running on pure adrenaline. He's doing things he shouldn't be able to do. He's also attempting things he shouldn't attempt."

"Do you think he'd go after Taperelli?"

"That was my first thought. I rushed men to his office, but he's gone for the day. I'm putting men on his house."

"Where is Herbie now?"

"I have no idea. But didn't Yvette show him that app?"

"Find My Phone?"

"Yeah. If we had his laptop, we could track him."

"And if we had his phone, we could find his laptop."

"Stone."

"Relax. It's probably at his apartment. I'm on my way."

Stone thundered down the stairs. "Fred!" he yelled.

99

Mario was skeptical. "You *don't* have the money?"

"I *have* the money. I don't have it now."

"That's the same as you don't have the money."

"Not at all. I have the money, and I will give it to you. Not next week. Not tomorrow. Today. I will give it to you today because today is payday and you are Mario Payday, and you are the one who gets paid."

"That is a lot of fancy talk for a man who doesn't have the money."

"Let me explain."

"I don't want to hear you explain. I just want the money."

"I quite understand. Do you understand? Your business, I mean. Do you understand your business?"

Carlo took a step toward Herbie, but Mario stopped him. "I understand my business perfectly. I do not need a lecture from you."

"You understand your business perfectly from your point of view. You don't understand it from mine. What kind of a guy borrows ninety thousand dollars from Mario Payday?"

"You didn't. You borrowed it from Vinnie the Vig."

"Exactly. And more to the point, what type of guy borrows ninety thousand dollars from Vinnie the Vig?"

"He'd have to be pretty desperate," Carlo said.

Mario gave him a look. It was bad enough listening to the guy's talk. He didn't need his own boys helping him.

"You've got to be a pretty bad risk to borrow from Vinnie the Vig," Herbie said. "You need to be at loose ends because the interest is going to kill you more often than not. To put yourself in that kind of hole, you must be a hard-core addict, the type of gambler who can never walk away from the table a winner because as long as he's got any cash at all, he's going to bet it. You know that type of guy? Of course you know that type of guy. That type of guy pays for all your fancy suits."

"I'm not amused, Mr. Fisher. You've got

two minutes before you're out the window again. I wouldn't waste them."

"You know what it's like with an addict. One drink, and they're back on the sauce. Or one hand of cards. Well, that's me, and that's how I ran through my money, and that's why I have a conservator. He was put in charge of clearing up all my past debts, and making sure I didn't accrue any present ones. Well, this is a past debt, and he has to honor it, which he is willing to do. The only problem is he won't give me the money."

"Hey," Carlo said, "what kind of runaround is this?"

Mario put up his hand. "Mr. Fisher, my boys are getting impatient. You say you can get the money, then you say you can't. While I certainly appreciate the circuitous logic you're spewing, if it does not end with me getting the money, it would be very unfortunate for all concerned."

"Of course you get the money, and you get it today. I'm just explaining why it isn't in my pocket. My conservator wouldn't give me ninety thousand dollars to pay you because he knows I am an addict, and you don't give ninety thousand dollars to an addict. He knows I'd go straight to the track."

"That would be most unwise, Mr. Fisher."

"To try to double my money before I paid you off? To an addict like me that would seem like the wisest thing in the world. But that's not going to happen because my conservator won't give the money to me, but he'll give it to you. Which frankly would be a big relief. I would like this matter resolved as much as you would. So what do you say? Let's go get it."

"Who is this conservator?"

"My uncle Henry, who was put in this position because he was a hard-nose, pain-in-the-ass stick-in-the-mud who won't make a move without a second or third opinion. You can be assured he has looked you up, knows you are who you say you are, knows you have a reputation, and knows you are not the type of man to forgive a debt. He has come to the conclusion that you have to be paid, though I must say, he is not happy about it."

"The happiness of your uncle is not my top priority."

"I understand. Unfortunately, it's one of mine." Herbie gestured to the door. "Shall we?"

Mario Payday frowned. "Are you sure Uncle Henry has the money?"

"I just got off the phone with him."

"Why can't he bring it to us?"

"He doesn't like traveling with that much cash."

"And yet he has it with him. That makes no sense."

"He lives near the bank," Herbie said. "He doesn't live near you."

Mario Payday took a puff on his cigar. He exhaled a billow of smoke and nodded to the goon who was his driver. "Bring the car around."

100

David's cabbie was getting antsy. "How much longer are we going to wait here?"

"Not much longer," David said, though of course he had no idea, and he was getting antsy himself. The meter kept clicking over, and while he could cover it with a credit card, keeping the cabbie happy might take a cash bribe, and he was low on cash.

There was a bank across the street.

"See that ATM? Hang in here. I'm going to get you some money."

David waited for the light to change, then hopped out of the cab and sprinted across the street. He swiped his card, punched in his security code, and took out four hundred dollars.

Herbie came out of the office building with two goons and a plump man with a mustache and a big cigar. A town car drove up to the door. They climbed into it and it took off.

David raced across the street, dodging a bus and a truck, jumped into the cab, and said, "That's him in the limo."

"You've got to be kidding."

David fanned the wad of twenties. "Drive, or I'm hopping out."

The cab took off.

101

Fred screeched the Bentley to a stop in front of Herbie's building. Stone hopped out and pointed his finger at the doorman. "I have to pick up Herbie's iPad. Give me his key."

The doorman knew he was a friend of Herbie's, had actually been there when Stone helped Herbie furnish the place. He gave him a key and sent him up. The hundred-dollar tip probably didn't hurt.

The iPad wasn't in Herbie's office, or in the living room, or in the bar. He eventually found it in the bedroom sitting on a bedside table next to a bottle of perfume and the latest issue of *Vogue.* Yvette's side of the bed. Stone wondered if Herbie had ever used the iPad himself.

Stone switched it on and opened the tracking app.

A light began blinking in the midst of a map.

Stone rang for the elevator and called Dino. "He's in Queens."

"Then he's not going after Taperelli. He lives in Jersey."

"Who's in Queens?"

"I have no idea, but I'm on my way."

"You calling the cops?"

"Not the local cops. Herbie wouldn't want that. I'm taking my best men."

"I'm one of them."

"I can't wait for you."

"Are you kidding me? I've got the iPad. Fred's double-parked out front. You'll be lucky if you keep up."

102

Melanie was weighing her odds, which she was hard-pressed to do because she was almost delusional with exhaustion and hunger. They hadn't been feeding her. She'd complained, but they hadn't given a damn. They clearly weren't prepared for keeping prisoners, or at least they weren't prepared for keeping one alive. No one knew where she was, including her, and no one was coming to help, and the options she'd rejected before were looking more and more attractive.

She thought about the window. Even if she could get it open — and that was a big *if* — would she be able to survive the fall and run far enough away to get help?

Was that a better chance than attacking a man on her way to the bathroom? It seemed a toss-up. They had their guns out now, each time they opened the door. Still, they wouldn't be expecting an attack, wouldn't realize how agile she was. Could she disarm an armed man?

She liked the idea better than the window, all that jagged glass slashing her to bits as she smashed her bones on the pavement below.

She'd do it the next time they took her to the bathroom. She'd hear the key in the lock and she'd be ready.

103

Taperelli was sitting in his large leather chair with his feet up and a drink in his hand. On a local chat show Jules Kenworth was pontificating on the benefits his new building would have for the community. To hear him talk, Jules Kenworth was almost single-handedly responsible for easing unemployment and bringing commerce to New York City.

Tommy Taperelli's wife stuck her head in the study door.

"Not now," Taperelli said irritably. His wife knew better than to disturb him in the study.

"There are cops outside. I thought you'd want to know."

Taperelli kicked his feet off the settee and spilled his drink. "What the hell!?"

He went to the window, lightly brushed aside a corner of the curtain, and looked outside.

Taperelli called Mookie. "I've got cops on my house."

"Oh?"

"So far they're just doing drive-bys, no one's knocked on the door. But they're staking the place out, so maybe someone talked and they're looking for the girl. If so, they're looking in the wrong place. They've got no reason to look in the *right* place, but be alert. You out there now?"

"Yeah."

"How many guys you got?"

"Me, Gus, Chico, and Lou."

"Everybody carrying?"

"Sure."

"Check on the girl."

Mookie hung up the phone and went upstairs. The door was closed, the key was in the lock.

Mookie raised his voice. "Back away from the door."

Mookie took his gun out, unlocked the door with his left hand, twisted the knob, and pushed the door open.

Melanie was standing by the door, close enough to have kicked him if he hadn't been wary. When she saw the gun in his hand she took a step back.

"That's a good girl," Mookie said.

"I have to go to the bathroom."

"Yeah, well, I'd like to win the lottery," Mookie said. He slammed the door and went downstairs to get a beer.

104

Dino swerved around a taxi with his cell phone plastered to his ear. He straightened the car, barked at Stone, "Where is he now?"

Stone was thrown sideways as Fred overtook a semi, skidded into the outer lane. "L.I.E., heading east toward City Field."

"Where are you?"

"About ten minutes behind."

"I'm catching up."

"Bullshit," Stone said. "Your only advantage is you don't have to worry about getting pulled over."

"You're sweating a speeding ticket?"

"I don't want to miss the action." Fred nosed the Bentley through a gap the size of a pinhole and floored the gas.

Herbie was crushed between Carlo and Ollie the Ox. With the town car this crowded, Mario Payday was sitting up front with the driver, leaving the others to the backseat.

Herbie didn't mind being squished, he was just afraid they'd notice his gun, or the damn thing would go off and he'd shoot himself in the leg. The gamble was desperate enough. He didn't need the attempt to be over before it began. The thug squishing his gun had so much fat and muscle he didn't seem to notice the hard metal jamming into his leg.

The town car took an exit. The turn jammed the gun even harder into the side of the thug.

Herbie tried to control his breathing, and prayed that Ollie the Ox lived up to his nickname.

The cab almost missed the exit. David had to scream at the driver, who nearly totaled the cab, causing a ten-car pileup that would have shut down the L.I.E. He cut across two lanes of traffic and fishtailed onto the exit ramp as a chorus of car horns applauded the move.

The cab was much too close to the car for comfort.

"Slow!" David warned. "In case the light's red."

It wasn't. The town car breezed right off the exit just as the light was changing.

"Make it! Make it! Make it!" David

screamed.

The cabbie missed the last flash of yellow and flew through on the red, prompting another blare of horns.

A block ahead, the town car appeared to take no notice. It slowed and took a right. The cabbie graced David with his ritual grumble, and followed.

105

Mario's town car pulled up in front of the house, and the four men got out and walked up to the door. Carlo banged on it. After a moment, he banged on it again.

Gus opened the door and peered out. His attitude was not welcoming. "Whaddya want?"

"Ninety thousand dollars," Carlo said.

Gus blinked. "What?"

"We're here for the money."

Gus laughed. "Get lost." He started to shut the door.

Carlo's eyes blazed. He moved his bulk forward into the doorway and started to draw his gun, but Mario Payday grabbed his arm. "Carlo. There is no need for unpleasantness. Let Mr. Fisher handle this." Mario pushed Herbie forward. "Mr. Fisher, if you please."

Herbie smiled at the two goons. "Could I speak to Uncle Henry, please?"

The man's brow furrowed. "Who?"

"He's expecting me. I know you're here to guard the money, but not from *me*. I'm the one the money is *for.*"

"Oh, is that right?"

"Yes, it is," Mario Payday said. He bulled his way in the door with his usual sense of entitlement, pushing Herbie along with him. Mario's goons crowded in behind him.

Cousin Lou, roused from his lethargy, got up from the couch. "Hey. This is my house."

"Are you Uncle Henry?" Mario said.

"I'm Cousin Lou."

Mookie came out of the kitchen with a beer. "Hey, what's going on here?" His eyes widened. "Mario Payday! What the hell are you doing here?" He spotted Herbie. "And the lawyer. What are you doing with *him*? I thought you killed his girlfriend."

Herbie blinked. His head came up. *Mario Payday* killed Yvette? Not Tommy Taperelli?

In a flash, he realized it was true.

There was no time for that now. The stairs were across the room. He had to get there. And here he was, trapped between two gangs of goons.

"He's got a gun!" Herbie warned.

No one had, but suddenly everyone did. No one fired, but everyone drew at once. The thugs faced each other down.

Herbie's gun was still in his hip holster. He surreptitiously eased it out and let it hang down the side of his leg.

He squeezed the trigger and fired a shot into the floor.

And everyone began shooting.

106

David stopped the cab two houses down from Cousin Lou's. He watched as Herbie and the men went up to the front door. As soon as they went inside, he began creeping up on the house. He'd just reached the front lawn when there was a single shot, followed by a hail of gunfire.

David jerked his cell phone out of his pocket and called 911.

Herbie dived for the floor, rolled over, and came up by the stairs. He crawled up them on his hands and knees as gunfire exploded all around him. He reached the top, stood up, and glanced around. Down the hall was a closed door with the key in the lock. He raced to it, twisted the key, and opened the door.

Melanie was quivering in fear as she heard a cacophony of gunfire from downstairs, but she wouldn't let herself succumb to panic. She had to defend herself, now more than ever.

In the midst of the shooting, she heard a heavy tread in the hallway approaching her room. She positioned herself in a loose crouch, hands up in fighting position, her whole body coiled and ready for action.

The key turned in the lock.

The door opened.

She reacted with as much speed as she could muster, kicking the man in the balls. He doubled over in agony. She recognized him just in time to stop from decking him with a haymaker.

"My God, Herbie! What are you doing here? What's happening?" Melanie said.

Herbie tried to answer but couldn't. He held up his hand, gulped for air. He managed to croak out, "We've got to get out of here."

David snuck up on the house, carefully, as shots were still ringing out. There was a window on the side where he could risk a look. He crept up to the house and raised himself on tiptoes.

The window exploded in a hail of glass as a body hurtled through it and landed in a heap on the lawn. It was a thug. He had a gun in his hand. He struggled to his feet and took off without a backward glance.

Mookie ran down the street full-tilt with his gun in his hand. He was lucky to be alive. He knew his men probably were not. He'd seen Gus go down. And Cousin Lou was right out in the open, too dumb to duck. But Mario Payday, a fucking loan shark, what the hell was a loan shark doing there anyway? And with the goddamned lawyer who was supposed to have given up and taken a dive. Jesus Christ, how did this all go south so quickly? Even if he got out of it, Tommy Taperelli would kill him.

A police car hurtled down the street, straight at him. Mookie raised the gun. Before he could fire, a second police car roared up. And a third. And a fourth. All stopped with their lights on him.

Policemen poured out of the cars. And a bullhorn, a fucking bullhorn, blared, "You're surrounded. Drop the gun."

Mookie's mouth fell open. My God, did cops really say that?

His gun fell from nerveless fingers.

Mookie raised his hands to the sky as cops swarmed around him.

107

Downstairs the gunfire had stopped. That could have meant anything, but there were no voices.

Herbie crept down the stairs ahead of Melanie. There were bodies everywhere. He couldn't tell if they were dead, but they were down. The three hoods from the house, and Carlo, and the driver, and Ollie the Ox. Melanie cringed slightly at the sight.

"Come on," Herbie said, helping her along. She passed him on the stairs, stepped over Gus's foot, and headed for the door.

Mario Payday came out of the kitchen with a gun in his hand.

Stone and Dino flew by the cops arresting Mookie, roared down the street, and screeched to a stop in front of Cousin Lou's house, the approaching sirens of the local cops close in their wake.

David Ross spotted them, waved his arms,

and pointed. "They're in there."

Stone recognized him as they hopped out of the cars. "What the hell?" he said without breaking stride.

"Who's that?" Dino yelled.

"My client," Stone yelled.

They raced up the walk.

Mario Payday's normally genial face twisted in rage. Herbie had set him up, tricked him, lured him into a trap, and got his men killed. Worse, *he hadn't paid him*! No one did that to Mario Payday.

Mario raised his gun and fired.

Herbie stepped in front of Melanie, taking the bullet in his chest. As he fell, he shot Mario Payday twice in the head as Stone and Dino burst in the door.

108

Donnie missed the news on TV. He'd avoided anyplace showing the local news, not wanting to be sitting there when his mug shot came on. He was sure someone would notice the resemblance. So he never saw the news that the police had a new suspect in Yvette's murder case. He thought he was still on the run from a murder rap.

Donnie dyed his hair. His beard wasn't working for him, at least it wasn't coming in fast enough, so he bought a box of hair dye at Duane Reade. He bought red dye, probably a mistake. Whether it was the consistency of his hair or he just didn't do it right, it came out blotchy, which was most unfortunate. He looked like the front man for an unsuccessful rock band.

He also bought a pair of glasses. He was going to get sunglasses, but he figured that would look suspicious. He was at that stage where he was second-guessing everything.

Glasses would be a disguise, but sunglasses would be a dead giveaway.

He found a rack of reading glasses in the drugstore and chose a pair with the largest rims and the weakest prescription. The pair he chose were of dark black plastic, and allowed him to get around without actually walking into walls. They still blurred his vision, which made it harder to spot imaginary dangers.

His money was running out, but he kept on the run. He just stumbled on with his red hair and Elton John–sized glasses, the Mr. Magoo of all burglars, a nearsighted circus clown.

109

Jules Kenworth was afraid of the call. Tommy Taperelli's empire had collapsed, and with it any chance of pressuring Councilman Ross on the vote. It was hard to believe. Two days ago they had the man's daughter, they had the man's son on trial, they had every ace in the deck, and then this two-bit pip-squeak lawyer beat them with a pair of deuces. Never mind kissing a quarter of a billion down the drain, Kenworth was liable to lose his status, his position in high society. He had seen it happen to others, but never thought it might happen to him. Dinner invitations fall off, phone calls aren't returned, and suddenly there you were, just another unimportant billionaire, a nameless, faceless statistic lost among the unimportant, unwashed, huddled masses that comprised the majority of the wealthy one percent.

But that wasn't the worst of it. Suddenly

there was the threat of jail, a very tangible prospect. Taperelli's men had been caught with the councilman's daughter, and one of them, the last man standing, was probably spilling his guts, citing chapter and verse and naming names. Did the guy know *his* name? How could he not? Kenworth's relationship with Taperelli was no secret. The acquaintance of a mob boss was a real feather in his cap. It had gotten him laid once, when his money hadn't — go figure — but he understood the allure. It was the Robin Hood appeal. Not that he'd ever given to the poor, but still. The idea of the bad boy. The glory that now was turning around to bite him.

Taperelli was going down, and Kenworth was in danger of going with him.

Kenworth dreaded the call.

The intercom buzzed.

The cheery voice of his secretary chirruped, "Taperelli on two."

Kenworth's pulse quickened. For a moment he wasn't sure what to do. Should he buzz his secretary back, tell her to say he wasn't there? No, he'd taken too long. Taperelli'd know he was. And what difference did it make? If Taperelli had rolled on him, he needed to know.

He just didn't want to hear.

Kenworth clicked the button and picked up the phone. "Hello?"

"Jules? Tommy. Listen, I just wanted to apologize."

"For what?" Kenworth said.

"What do you mean, for what? For letting it all get away from me."

"Ah, well, what you gonna do?"

"I know, I know." There was a pause, then, "Listen. You know Mookie's talking."

"Oh?"

"Yeah, he's giving the cops everything, and that's not good. He knows about our relationship, and he was caught out there with the girl. Well, not with the girl, but running away from the house. He's admitting to grabbing the councilman's daughter, and telling Kelly to set up his son, and the whole bit. I don't know how much of it is going to stick, because there's no corroborating testimony, everyone else is dead, which, I hate to say it, but it's like we caught a break. The point is, none of this should come back on you. You never dealt with Mookie, so anything he spills about you is hearsay. And I'm not going to spill the beans. So you can rest easy.

"Me, not so much. I probably got some courtroom proceedings coming up. I'll probably be running up some astronomical legal fees, and I might need you to help me out in that department, but the point is you won't be spending them on yourself.

"Anyway, that's the situation. I'll let you know how it pans out."

Kenworth hung up the phone and slumped back in his chair. Relief flooded over him. Taperelli was a brick. He could count on their relationship. Oh, yeah, there was the incidental request for legal fees, with the implied threat of what he might say if they were not forthcoming, but that was nothing compared to what it could have been.

Kenworth sighed and poured himself a snifter of cognac.

Yup, he'd dodged a bullet.

Tommy Taperelli hung up the phone. "How was that?"

The police detective took off his headset. "Not bad for a first pass. I don't think he suspected a thing." He pointed over at the technician manning the recorder. "Good for sound?"

The technician nodded, gave him an A-OK sign.

"Wait a minute. First pass?" Tommy said.

"Sure. Next time it will be easy. You can

listen to this back, see where you can improve."

"You didn't say anything about a next time."

The detective glanced over at the assistant district attorney, who had been sitting back and observing the proceedings. The ADA placed his set of headphones on the table and smiled patronizingly. "Mr. Taperelli, do you want this deal or not? It's not how much you cooperate, or how many phone calls you have to make, or who those phone calls are to. The question is, do you want to play ball? If you do, it's our game. It's our game because we already have one gangster spilling his guts. Kidnapping and extortion are a slam-dunk, and murder's on the table, and the only reason you have any wiggle room at all is that Jules Kenworth is a bigger fish. Only if you don't hook the bigger fish, suddenly *you're* the bigger fish, and all bets are off. Your lawyer understands that, Mr. Taperelli, and if you don't understand that you should have a talk with him because, trust me, you are going to be making as many phone calls as we like."

110

Herbie groaned and opened his eyes.

"Ah, look who decided to join the party," Stone said.

Herbie blinked. He was in a hospital bed. He had no idea how he got there. "What happened?"

"You shot it out with the mob," Dino said. "They're all dead, except one guy we picked up running away."

"Mario Payday's?"

"Taperelli's."

"Right. Mario's men are down."

"So is he. Took two shots in the head. Does that ring any bells?"

"Melanie?"

"She's fine," Stone said. "She doesn't have a bullet in her. She's the only one who didn't."

"Why'd you go cowboy on us?" Dino said.

"Give me a break. They'd have killed her had I gotten the police involved. With a dirty cop in Taperelli's pocket, who can you trust?"

"Me," Dino said. "You don't think I can be discreet?"

"You'd have stopped me."

"You're damn right I would. You know how long you were on the operating table? That bullet lodged pretty close to your heart."

"It was her only chance."

"Getting yourself shot?"

"Bringing in Mario Payday. That made it a mob thing, not a cop thing. It confused the situation enough that they didn't have a chance to kill the girl."

"See, Dino," Stone said, "I told you. He didn't think you could do it."

"He's loopy on pain pills. He doesn't know what he's saying."

Melanie burst into the room. "They told me you woke up!" She started to throw herself into his arms, and stopped. "They said not to agitate you."

Stone and Dino exchanged glances.

"Are you okay?" Herbie asked.

"Am *I* okay? You're the one who got shot."

Herbie smiled gamely. "Hadn't noticed."

David Ross and his father pushed in next.

"They said you woke up," David said. "How do you feel?"

"Like I missed a court date," Herbie said. "Did we get a continuance?"

Councilman Ross smiled. "You've been out longer than you think. Detective Kelly's under investigation. All charges against David have been dropped."

"Really?" Herbie said.

"The goon we picked up fleeing was Taperelli's man at the courthouse," Dino said. "He knew the whole setup. He's giving us anything he can think of."

"How come?"

"You don't rat on Taperelli and live. The guy's only hope is Taperelli takes a long fall. He'll do anything he can to make that happen."

There was too much going on for Herbie, and too many people in the room. He needed some of them to leave. No one seemed about to, so he tuned them out in his head.

"So, Melanie . . ." he began.

A young man pushed his way into the room. He was well-dressed, handsome, and amiable. "I finally parked the car." He saw Herbie and said, "There he is. The man of the hour, Melanie's savior, and our hero." He walked over to the bed, put his arm around Melanie, and held her close. "We can't thank you enough."

"Herbie," Melanie said, "this is Arthur, my fiancé. He flew in from the coast when he heard."

Herbie forced a smile. "You're a lucky man."

"Lucky you were there. I can't imagine what might have happened."

"I could, every day," Melanie said. "But it's over now."

"Let's leave Herbie to get some rest," the councilman said. He herded the others out of the room, leaving only Stone and Dino.

Stone watched them go. "Tough break," he said.

"What do you mean?" Herbie said.

"You know what I mean. Nice girl."

The phone rang.

Dino scooped it up. "Hello? . . . Oh, hi." He covered the phone. "Bill Eggers."

Herbie winced. "I'm too groggy to talk. Take a message."

Dino relayed the information. It didn't go over well. He got an earful. Eventually he hung up the phone.

"What's that all about?" Herbie said.

"As long as you're going to live, he wants you back at work. Something about a corporate merger."

Herbie groaned. He shook his head and chuckled. "Want to stop his heart? Call him back and tell him now that I've had a taste of it, I prefer trial work."

Stone nodded approvingly. "You're a cruel man. I like that."

Herbie grinned. "Wait! I've got a better idea."

"Oh?"

"Fair is fair." Herbie cocked his head. "Tell him to give it to James Glick."

111

James Glick looked longingly across the border.

On the other side was Mexico, the land of life, liberty, and the happiness of no pursuit. He figured they wouldn't come after him there. It was an irrational notion, born of fear, but one to which he clung desperately.

In his left hand was the passport the man in Mexicali had made him for a hundred dollars. It looked real. There was no reason for anyone to doubt it. His picture stared up from it, and all the information on it was absolutely accurate, except for the passport number and expiration date. No one would be apt to check them. The man who made the passport had assured him they would not. Of course, he'd been eager to make a hundred bucks.

James Glick pushed his way out of the shadows toward the line of people waiting to cross the border.

Two men came out of the shadows, grabbed him by the arms, and pulled him away.

No one tried to help him. No one even stepped out of line. A couple of men shook their heads dispiritedly and went back to what they were doing.

James Glick was terrified, but not surprised. It only seemed natural, somehow, that it would end like this, that he would be snatched away from the goal line with victory in sight.

The two men pulled him back into the shadows.

"James Glick."

He nearly peed in his pants. It was the two men he'd seen in the Marriott. The men with guns.

"No. You have me confused with someone else."

"Yeah. We probably have you confused with this guy." He pulled a photo out of his jacket pocket. It was a head shot of James Glick taken from the Woodman & Weld website, listing him as one of their criminal attorneys. He shoved it in Glick's face. "We probably confused you with him because you look close enough to be his twin brother."

James Glick was terrified. "Please. I didn't

do anything. I swear it."

"If only that were true, Mr. Glick, we would not have had to chase you all over the damn country. But you did, and we did, and we got you."

"Please, I didn't do anything. I swear."

"Good thing you're not under oath, or you'd pile up another charge. As it is, we got you for conspiring to commit a crime, conspiring to conceal a crime, failure to appear in court, crossing I-lost-count-of-how-many state lines in order to evade arrest, and the list goes on. All in all, Mr. Glick, I would not like to be you."

James Glick blinked. "Arrest?"

"Did you think we were going to let you walk after all the trouble you made? Even if you agreed to come back, we know your word's no good for anything. I must say, I don't envy you your choices. What are you going to do, serve time or testify against Tommy Taperelli? You happen to be in luck in that a lot of his muscle's dead and they might need your testimony. Still, it's not a pretty prospect."

The detective turned him around and snapped handcuffs on his wrists.

James Glick had never felt so happy in his life.

AUTHOR'S NOTE

I am happy to hear from readers, but you should know that if you write to me in care of my publisher, three to six months will pass before I receive your letter, and when it finally arrives it will be one among many, and I will not be able to reply.

However, if you have access to the Internet, you may visit my website at www .stuartwoods.com, where there is a button for sending me e-mail. So far, I have been able to reply to all my e-mail, and I will continue to try to do so.

If you send me an e-mail and do not receive a reply, it is probably because you are among an alarming number of people who have entered their e-mail address incorrectly in their mail software. I have many of my replies returned as undeliverable.

Remember: e-mail, reply; snail mail, no reply.

When you e-mail, please do not send attachments, as I never open them. They can take twenty minutes to download, and they often contain viruses.

Please do not place me on your mailing lists for funny stories, prayers, political causes, charitable fund-raising, petitions, or sentimental claptrap. I get enough of that from people I already know. Generally speaking, when I get e-mail addressed to a large number of people, I immediately delete it without reading it.

Please do not send me your ideas for a book, as I have a policy of writing only what I myself invent. If you send me story ideas, I will immediately delete them without reading them. If you have a good idea for a book, write it yourself, but I will not be able to advise you on how to get it published. Buy a copy of *Writer's Market* at any bookstore; that will tell you how.

Anyone with a request concerning events or appearances may e-mail it to me or send it to: Publicity Department, Penguin Random House LLC, 375 Hudson Street, New York, NY 10014.

Those ambitious folk who wish to buy film, dramatic, or television rights to my books should contact Matthew Snyder, Creative Artists Agency, 9830 Wilshire Boulevard, Beverly Hills, CA 98212-1825.

Those who wish to make offers for rights of a literary nature should contact Anne Sibbald, Janklow & Nesbit, 445 Park Avenue, New York, NY 10022. (Note: This is not an invitation for you to send her your manuscript or to solicit her to be your agent.)

If you want to know if I will be signing books in your city, please visit my website, www.stuartwoods.com, where the tour schedule will be published a month or so in advance. If you wish me to do a book signing in your locality, ask your favorite bookseller to contact his Penguin representative or the Penguin publicity department with the request.

If you find typographical or editorial errors in my book and feel an irresistible urge to tell someone, please write to Sara Minnich at Penguin's address above. Do not e-mail your discoveries to me, as I will already have learned about them from others.

A list of my published works appears on my website. All the novels are still in print in paperback and can be found at or ordered from any bookstore. If you wish to obtain hardcover copies of earlier novels or of the two nonfiction books, a good used-book store or one of the online bookstores can help you find them. Otherwise, you will have to go to a great many garage sales.

ABOUT THE AUTHORS

Stuart Woods is the author of more than sixty-five novels, including the *New York Times*–bestselling Stone Barrington and Holly Barker series. He is a native of Georgia and began his writing career in the advertising industry. *Chiefs*, his debut in 1981, won the Edgar Award. An avid sailor and pilot, Woods lives in Florida, Maine, and New Mexico.

Parnell Hall is an actor, screenwriter, singer/songwriter, and the author of more than forty novels. He was awarded the Eye Lifetime Achievement Award from the Private Eye Writers of America, and has been a finalist for an Edgar, two Lefty, and three Shamus awards. Hall lives in New York City.